# Wilhelm the Lemming:

# How I was Dethroned and Became Emperor.

A novel

By

W.R.L. Battle

This narrative is a work of fiction. Names, characters, places and incidents are either the product of the author's imagination or are used fictitiously, any resemblance to actual persons living or dead, business establishments, events, or locals are completely coincidental.

Wilhelm the Lemming: How I was Dethroned and Became Emperor

Copyright © 2021 by Wesley Robert Battle

Cover Art © 2021 by Wesley Robert Battle

Cover Art by Gary T. Val

All Rights Reserved. This literary work may not be reproduced in any form by any means whatsoever without written permission.

ISBN 978-0-578-92178-5 (Paperback)

ISBN: 978-0-578-93762-5 (eBook)

To:

Dylan Cuddington

And

Alexander Tryciecky

For making History come to life.

# Chapter 1

Well, hello! If you're reading this book, then you probably want to know how I got dethroned, and how I became emperor of Rulksferd. If that's not the case, then you're probably desperate for some entertainment. Before I took my rightful place as king, I was living the high life. When you're the youngest of four brothers in the royal family, there's not much for you to do other than party, play games, and lying about soaking up the sun. I had it all figured out back then. I would never be king, and that was alright with me. But unfortunately, as you probably have guessed, I became king.

My first brother, Wilhelm I, died of a heart attack riding the merry-go-round. My second brother, Wilhelm II, was captured by pirates and was never heard from again. Finally, my third brother, Wilhelm III, got all religious and became a monk. Now that I think about it, I should have tagged along with him. Living in a monastery for the rest of my life would have been a whole lot better than ruling an entire nation.

I was the only one of my father's sons to be there for his last moment on Earth. With the help of a few servants, he lifted up his sword and dubbed me King of Rulksferd. Now, no disrespect to my father or anything - he probably had no choice in the matter – but I wanted to rid myself of the title as soon as I could. So, I had a plan that would do just that.

I hired an assassin named Dorvell Timus. He was an old raccoon, with weathered fur, and a puss like substance in his left eye. We secretly met in a tavern on the outskirts of the kingdom. I paid him five hundred gold coins up front, and I gave him the rundown on how I wanted him to kill me. Once I took my place on the throne, he was supposed to send an arrow straight to my forehead. I warned him that if he got caught, I wouldn't have his back, and he seemed to understand.

Inauguration day came, and I was ready. The bishop placed the crown on my head, and I sat down on my throne waiting for the arrow to take me away. But unfortunately, the fool missed by a long shot, several times in fact. He was caught by the guards and executed on the very same day.

Upset with his failure, I came up with a more ingenious plan. If I was going to be king, then I was going to be the worst king Rulksferd had ever seen! They would have no choice but to dethrone me. For the first week or so I made up so many laws, I guess you could say I lost track.

It was all put to an end when my advisors showed up in my throne room five weeks into my reign. Rudding, a beaver, came out of the crowd and spoke up.

"Sire," he said with all his strength, "The people are not happy at all with what you've been doing."

"They're rioting in the streets!" shouted one advisor.

"They want your head on a silver platter!" said another.

"They want you dethroned!" shouted another one.

"I think I'm in the wrong meeting," someone stated.

"Well, I tried," I said giving a false sigh, "I guess I'm not cut out to be a ruler. I've brought shame to my family name."

"What do you suppose we do?" asked Rudding.

"I don't know," I replied, "You're a bunch of smart guys, just come up with something."

They all gasped. A sight of dread formed on their faces, except, oddly enough, Rudding's.

"What's wrong?" I asked.

"Guards seize him!" shouted Rudding pointing his finger at me.

"Hey!" I said confused, "What'd I do?"

"Alright, what seems to be the problem here?" said one of the guards.

"The king said we're a bunch of smart guys!" answered Rudding.

"Yep, that's a violation of Decree 165421047-3," replied the guard, "By order of King Wilhelm IV, referring to the royal advisors as a bunch of 'smart guys' is punishable by life in prison."

"But I'm the king!" I shouted at the guard, "You can't do this to me!"

"Sorry, my Lord," the guard replied, "No one's above the law, including you."

With that, he grabbed me by the shoulders and dragged me down to the royal jail. He pushed me with such force that my crown fell off of my head. I wanted to live a life outside the kingdom, not in its prison. He unlocked the jail door and tossed me, as if I were a ragdoll, into a black abyss. I landed on the damp, cold, and filthy floor with a thud. The door closed behind me.

I ran to the door, jumped towards the window, and fruitlessly tried to rip the bars out with my bare paws.

"Get me out of here!" I demanded as I watched the guard walk away, "I'm innocent I tell ya! This is all a misunderstanding!"

"Get in line bub," replied a voice behind me. I turned around. What I saw made me lose my grip on the bars and I landed on the ground a second time.

It seemed like hundreds of animals throughout the kingdom were all crammed into the entire room.

"How did you guys get in here?" I asked them.

"King Wilhelm has gone blooming mad, that's what!" replied a chubby possum with clothes too small for his own body, "I'm in here because I'm too fat. So, what if I have a weight problem? I'm doing nothing wrong!"

"I'm in here because I whistled on a Tuesday," replied a fox, "What's so bad about whistling on a Tuesday? Why can't I whistle whenever I want to?"

"I said hello to my best friend when I met him at school today," replied a young muskrat, "Now I'll never see him, or my ma and pa, again."

"What are you in here for?" asked the fat possum.

"Oh, I called the royal advisors a bunch of smart guys." I replied.

"It doesn't make any sense," said an old rat, "Why would King Wilhelm do this?"

"I told ya, he's lost his blooming marbles!" replied the fat possum.

"When I get my paws on him, he'll be good as dead!" said a hedgehog.

"Here, here!" a bunch of animals replied.

"So, any plans on how to get out of here?" I asked. Silence followed.

"Alright," I said, "I guess it's all up to me."

After pondering for what seemed like several hours, I finally came up with a complicated and sophisticated plan to break everyone out of this scum hole. I got everyone together and told them what I had conjured up. They all liked my idea.

"Alright, any questions?" I asked concluding my instructions.

"Do we get to kill the king?" asked the hedgehog.

"Sure, why not?" I said knowing I would be long gone before they realized who I really was, "Alright let's do this, now I'll need. . ."

The prison wall behind us burst into a wave of bricks. A black sphere smashed through the prison door sending wooden debris flying everywhere. When the commotion settled, we all looked where the spherical shape had come from.

Apparently, a group of rebelling peasants got a hold of a cannon mounted on the castle wall and decided to shoot all around the castle.

"VIVA LE REVELOTION!" they yelled at the top of their lungs.

Without a second thought, everyone made a mad dash through the hole in the door. I was literally swept off my feet by the tidal wave of citizens.

"Find the king!" they chanted.

I was pushed by the current, this way and that. I tried pushing back, but they were too strong. Like a gush of water breaking through a dam, they all broke down the door into the royal throne room.

Near my throne a chalkboard stood with several words and markings on it. Some of the words were "anarchy", "democratic", "republic", "empire", "oligarchy" and so on and so forth.

"What's going on?" asked Rudding, "Don't you know we're voting for a new form of government here!?"

"Where's the king?" asked one voice.

"We want to purge his eyeballs out, wrap his intestines on a stake, and drown him to death with his own blood!" said an angry female voice.

Rudding looked at me, I silently begged him not to turn me in, but his deathly smile made me realize it was all in vain.

"Why, he's right there!" he replied.

"Where?" they asked.

Rudding grabbed the crown off the floor and said, "Why, right... here."

He walked towards me and placed the crown on my head. Everyone gasped before looking at me with rage burning in their eyes.

"N-n-now guys, let's don't be too hasty." I said slowly backing away, "A-a-after all, I want-ted to g-g-get out of prison j-just like you guys."

"We understand," said the young muskrat.

"You do?" I asked.

He smiled at me and then said, "Nope."

Someone pointed their fingers at me and yelled, "GET HIM!"

I turned around and ran as fast as I could. I ran down the stairs, ran out of the castle, ran past the courtyard, and ran outside the gate. I ran so fast my crown fell off my head a couple of miles back. I ran so fast, I didn't have time to think of Rudding's random act of betrayal. What did I ever do to him to make him want to do that? I ran so fast I didn't know where I was anymore, and I didn't even want to stop, unless I wanted to face the angry mob behind me.

# Chapter ii

My legs were cramped up; my head was sweating like crazy. My mouth was desperately craving for water by the second. I slowed down to a snail's pace. I looked to my left, and there was sand. I looked to my right, more sand. I turned around degrees, sand, sand and more sand.

"Ah, great!" I said to myself. I was in the middle of nowhere.

Thoughts of dread entered my mind. I didn't want my life to end this way. I was supposed to live the rest of my days in a paradise, not in a wasteland. The temptation to just collapse in the sand became more inviting every second, but I just had to keep walking. Maybe just a few miles or so, there would be an oasis or an inn.

With each step I took, the more my hopes were being shattered. I was dreading for my impending doom of going crazy before the vultures above tore me to shreds. I saw a little rocky mountain range in the distance. I didn't care whether it was a figment of my imagination or not, the mountain would provide a nice place to rest for the night.

I almost didn't make it, but thanks to the tiny bit of strength left, I was finally able to reach the foot of the mountain. I laid my back against the rocks. My concerns moved to refreshing myself with water. The very thought of it made my weak tongue leap with joy.

I made a short walk around the canyon to see if there was a river or something behind it. To my utter disappointment, there wasn't any sign of a drop of liquid anywhere. Even with the shade from the mountain, I was still going to die.

With nowhere to run and nowhere to find water, I was furious with myself.

"Wilhelm, you idiot!" I shouted to myself. "You no good, treacherous, evil fiend. ..."

The ground started to shake. I lost my balance and fell tail first into the sand. I looked to see what was happening. A large stone on the wall of the mountain started to roll back! In a few seconds, the ground stopped rumbling, and I could make out a little cave within the mountain.

"Well, what do you know," I said amazed. With no other option available, I walked into the deep and moist cave. I looked behind me, only to watch the stone roll back over the opening. The sound of the rock resting in place, reminded me of the final closing of a coffin. I was doomed to wander in the ominous cave for the rest of my life, with no hope of escape.

My hands caressed the wall, carefully putting one step in front of the other. I tried whistling a happy tune, but my own fearfulness made the tune in a mad scrambling of notes.

*"Don't worry,"* I said to myself, "At least nobody can find me here.*"*

It was then when my ears picked up, and my bone-dry tongue snapped to life. I rushed with all my strength to get one droplet into my mouth. After stumbling in the dark for a short time, I could finally make out the stalactites. Then I stuck out my tongue anticipating the sweet, cold sensation only water could bring.

I never knew how tasty water could be! I could have been there with my mouth opened wide for hours, but a bright yellow light in the distance got my attention. I was so busy trying to find water, I barely noticed it.

*"*I can't believe it!*"* I said, "There's an exit out of this cave after all!*"*

The closer I got to the yellow light, the brighter it became. I stopped to take in the view.

On the downside it wasn't an exit from the cave, but on the positive side I hit the jackpot! Mountains and mountains of gold and jewels as far as the eye could see.

It was as if I had died and gone to heaven. It made me happy for being kicked out of my own kingdom, it made me gleefully forget that one of my advisors backstabbed me, and it made me overjoyed of how lucky I was to stumble across such a place.

Just when I thought nothing could amaze me any further, I was proven wrong. In the middle of the room was a giant, solid gold throne resting on the widest golden stage I had ever seen. It was so awe inspiring, it made my throne look like a cheap wooden chair .

It was practically calling my name.

*"Wilhelm!"* I imagined it saying, *"Please sit on me! I've been waiting for eons just to feel the warm feeling of your royal tooshy!"*

It didn't have to tell me twice. After all, what's the point of a throne if nobody sat on it? With a mad dash, I zoomed by the stock piles of valuables, jumped over the two golden stairs, breezed over the goldish stage, and rested my butt on the god-like throne.

"Now this was a throne I could rule on!" I said satisfied with myself, "No father to compete with, no advice from pesky advisors, no annoying peasants who want my head on a silver platter, just me, me, me."

I couldn't explain it. I was happy. I had everything I ever wanted, but I was feeling a cold sensation that could only be described as an ever-expanding hole of emptiness inside me. I thought living a life of pleasure and having riches was all I needed to be happy. Yet, right then and there, I realized how wrong I was.

I cursed myself for going into the cave and not staying outside in the desert. At least in the desert I wouldn't die with the feeling of loneliness. The harsh sand and heat could have cared less if I died or not, but the gems and golden plates would mock me with the reflections of my own demise.

*"Look! It's the royal King Wilhelm!" they said in unison, before giving a fur raising laugh.*

*"Stop it!" I begged.*

*"What?" they asked grinning from side to side, "All the money in the world ain't good enough for ya?"*

*"I don't know," I confessed, "I don't know." I got off the throne as quickly as I could, but I must have stepped on the wrong paw or something because, with a*

*loud thud, I found myself face first on the golden stage. It was a great struggle, but I finally got myself back on my paws.*

*"Should have figured that out before you came in here!" said the objects,*

*I walked down the stairs. A jewel gave me a dirty look.*

*"What's the matter?" it asked with an evil grin, "Are you a coward?"*

*"No!" I exclaimed.*

*The piles started to grow thicker and thicker. With enough time, I reasoned, I would be suffocated to death! With that I started to run towards the exit.*

*"You can't take responsibility!" a chest proclaimed.*

*"You blame others, when you should be blaming yourself!" a statue accused. I was running down the aisle so fast, I could feel each pump my heart made.*

*"Yeah, run little lemming," said a bar of gold, "Run away, like the selfish coward you are!"*

*From what seemed like out of nowhere, a mirror suddenly fell two inches in front of me, blocking my path. My reflection gave a sinister smirk. "You're nothing but a selfish, spoiled, pampered, good-for-nothing brat, who never deserved to have been born in the first place!" it said before laughing maniacally.*

*"Shut up, you monster!" I exclaimed.*

*"I'm sorry, who locked up innocent animals just because he didn't want to be king?" it asked mockingly, "Who's the real monster here?"*

*I had no time to entertain it with an answer. The piles were growing at rapid rate, making the path thinner and thinner. With a quick rush, I leaped over the mirror and headed for the exit. A painting of my father toppled down the pile and landed right in front of my face. His soul crushing eyes glared at me.*

*I tripped and fell flat on my face. I couldn't get up in time. Diamonds consumed my paws, and gold coins forced themselves down my throat. The last thing I heard was the chanting of "Coward" hammering into my skull.*

*I fell down to the ground, to wait for the embracement of death.*

*The whole cave shook with the objects chanting "Coward, coward, coward!"*

# CHAPTER iii

"Help us," I heard a distant, soft voice cry out from the distance. I opened my eyes, only to realize that I never had left the golden throne.

"Who said that?" I asked scanning the piles of gold, "If you want to mock me, I can do that myself, thank you very much."

"Over here," said the voice, "Help us."

I cautiously got off the throne, slowly walked down the stairs, and crept towards to where I thought the voice was coming from. The treasure piles didn't move, and I preferred it that way.

"Where are you?" I asked louder.

"Come closer," said the voice, louder this time, "Hurry, there's no time to waste!"

"Just keep talking," I yelled out.

"What do you want us to say?" it asked, the voice sounded really close, almost as if it was behind the nearest stash in front of me.

"Anything," I replied, "Until I find you."

"Well we're really old, if that helps any," it said. "We've been captured by dangerous thieves, no doubt they are planning something nefarious."

"Okay?" I said questioning what I was even doing. None of this was making any sense. What if I was still dreaming? If I was still dreaming I figured it'd be best to play a long, for I was curious where this was going.

"Anything else?" I walked behind the pile, only to be dumbfounded with what I saw.

On a golden table, there lied a chandelier like structure. There were six of what looked like candle holders, but instead of pointing down they were pointed upwards. Instead of holding candles, four were holding diamonds – blue, white, yellow, and green – while the remaining two holders had nothing.

"Well, you're looking right at us," the voice said, while the blue diamond glowed in sync with every syllable.

"Oh, wait a minute," I said coming to a revelation, "I'm still asleep."

"I'm afraid you're not," said the blue diamond.

"Oh, no, no," I said shaking my head, "Watch, all I have to do is pinch myself, and I'll be sitting on the golden throne. Alright, here goes nothing! 3...2...1..."

I closed my eyes and gave myself the sharpest pinch to my fur as I could. I opened my eyes, only to see that I was still standing in front of the chandelier like object.

"Told ya," snapped the blue diamond.

"How can this be?" I asked horrified of the object, "Talking diamonds only exists in fairy tales!"

"We can explain later," said the blue diamond, "But you must free us."

"Yes," said the green diamond, "Free us before they come back."

"But I don't know what you guys are," I exclaimed. "I mean I know you're a bunch of diamonds, but how do I know if you were placed in there for a reason? I might as well be releasing a reign of terror on the land."

"Please," said the white diamond, "You'll just have to trust us."

"But . . ." I was about to say when I heard something outside the cave.

"You idiot!" exclaimed the voice from outside, "You darn, no good, treacherous, evil fiend!"

The ground started to shake, and a blinding light blasted through the opening of the cave.

"The thieves," exclaimed the yellow diamond, "Hide before they find you!"

With a jump and a dash, I hid behind a wooden treasure chest right next to the chandelier like object.

I slowly peaked above the treasure chest, only to quickly bring my face down. An entire line of scrawny, bone skinny animals wearing black robes were carrying all their loot only to dump it into one pile on a rough empty space on the cave's floor.

Hiding behind the bulky treasure chest, allowed me to conjure up a plan. All I had to do was wait for the thieves to fall asleep, sneak past the guards, get to the cave's entrance, say the magic words, and bingo, I would be home free! All I had to do was wait, and wait, and wait.

The sounds of precious treasure falling to the ground suddenly stopped, only to be replaced by a rough booming voice seconds later.

"My fellow thieves!" said the rough voice, "Our raid to Trestova, was a success!"

Cheers followed. I was about to wonder where Trestova was, but then the voice continued.

"We have gathered many treasures," the voice continued, "But this one, as you know, has more value than all the others."

*Ooohs* and *ahhhs* filled the room. I wanted to see what was so valuable, but I didn't want to risk getting caught.

"All we need is one more, and I... I mean we, will rule the world!" the voice shouted.

Thunderous shouts and applauses shook the very walls of the cave. It didn't take me long to put two and two together.

*Wilhelm, you ole chap* I thought to myself *What the heck have you gotten yourself in to?*

My thoughts were interrupted when I heard paw-steps coming towards me. Was my cover blown already? No. I saw a paw pressing a red emerald onto the holder, before moving away from my sight.

"Hey boss," I heard a nasally voice say, "Some of the men were wondering, since we're so close, can we have a celebration?"

"Have I allowed the men to celebrate before?" the rough voice asked.

"No sir," the nasally voice replied.

"What makes you think I would allow a celebration now?" the rough voice yelled angrily.

The animal with the nasally voice stuttered in fright for a second or two, before the rough voice gave a blood churning cackle.

"You guys are so easy to fool," the rough voice said gasping for air, before clearing his throat.

"Gentlemen," he continued, "To commemorate our one step toward world domination, drink, eat, and be merry!"

Voices of merriment followed.

"But," he said, bringing a halt to the thunderous commotion, "Make sure you are all sober for the ceremony tomorrow, and alert enough to be informed about our next raid. May the celebration begin!"

I couldn't believe my luck. Those thieves would be tipsy-turvey drunk sooner or later. All I had to wait for one of them to pass out, so I could take their clothes, put them on. I could head straight out of the cave wit no-one else was noticing.

I waited once again. The more I waited, the more certain I was that this plan was going to work. My chance to escape came sooner than I expected. A small tubby thief, in a drunken stupor, crashed right into the chest I was hiding behind, and fell face first on to the ground below.

I sneaked around the chest, and, when I thought no one was looking, quickly moved his body behind it. I carefully took off his black robes, black turban and black mask. Thaste, I put them onto myself. Part one of my plan was completed, all that was left to do was high tail it out of there.

I walked in front of the chest, to see the cave filled with other thieves wearing the same clothes I was wearing. Some were dancing, some were playing with their stolen goods, some were singing drinking songs, and some were just drinking the night away.

"Now sir," I heard the blue diamond say, "Free us."

"But, I still don't know what you little things are," I replied to them as indiscreetly as I could.

"We'll explain later," the diamond replied, "Just take us away from here."

To my luck, I found a few pockets in which I could hide the diamonds. I secretly snatched one diamond at a time, until I hid the red diamond.

"Alright," I said to the diamond, "Now, we're off!"

"Wait sir," said the blue diamond, "Get the lamp, get the lamp!"

"What lamp?" I asked, only to look at a golden oil lamp lying on the table that held the chandelier.

"Oh," I said in frustration, "Might as well ask to me to take all the treasure in this cave."

I snatched the lamp and stuffed it in my robes.

"Alright," I said with a sigh, "We're off, for real now."

Blending into the whole horde of drunken thieves was easier than I thought. As long as I had the black mask covering my mouth, I was good as gold. The only real struggle was avoiding an unwanted invite to be a part of a mass conga line.

It wasn't long until I was back to the stalactites from earlier, and I was just a few feet from where the giant boulder was.

"And where do you think you're going?" I heard the same rough voice say.

*Don't worry, Wilhelm* I thought to myself *Just play it cool.*

I turned around to see a tall ferret, with eyes angry enough they could light a candle, a mustache with points sharp enough to be used as daggers, and eyebrows as thick as bricks. He wore a black turban on his head with a red band going around the middle. His mask was off, revealing his scruffy black beard.

"I am needing to take a whizz," I said pretending to be drunk, "Fig'red I could go ou'side and drain the ole bladder."

I gave out a heavy laugh.

"Why not in here?" the ferret asked, "We're all the same here, just do your business."

"Oh, I'm s'rry," I apologized trying to think of an excuse, "I'm... I'm... wee shy. Yes, I can't do it fer an audience. So, don't mind me I'll j'st see meself out."

I was about to say the magic words but the guy stopped me.

"What's your name?" he asked.

"Me name is Methoosla Gremickle," I said, figuring he wouldn't know every thief in his group.

"Are you sure about that?" he asked moving towards me, "I've memorized every name here, and I don't remember any *Methoosla Gremickle*."

"I must 'ave forgot who I was then," I said trying to get him off my case.

"You know what else?" he asked, "I've also memorized everyone's voice here, and I don't think I've heard your voice before."

"Must be coming down wit' a cold," I said before giving a fake cough. In a flash, he pinned me to the wall with his paws. I was so scared I could barely move a strand of fur.

"Are you saying I'm wrong?" he growled, "I'm never wrong!"

He then moved his paws on to my robe.

"What's this?" he asked.

"Oh, t'is?" I asked frozen in fear, "I've grown a lump on me chest, the size of a walnut it is. I might not have much longer to live."

"You're right about that," said the ferret giving an evil grin.

"I am?" I asked wondering what he would do next.

"Anyone who steals from me," the ferret replied taking diamond out of my robe, "Will be sentenced to death!"

# CHAPTER iV

There I was, tied to a wooden chair with eyes full of rage surrounding me. It was **bad** enough that I tried to get away with stealing from them, but I was in a whole other world of pain when I was the reason their source of drunken merriment came to an end. I sighed in spite of myself. Guess it was my destiny to ruin everything I came across.

"So, who are you, really?" the ferret asked looking at me straight in the eye.

"I was going to ask you the same question," I remarked.

"Good enough," he said growling, "My name is Dhikrullah (De-crew-la) Alasar, Master of Thieves, Terror of the East, Destroyer of Villages and Robber of Widows. Now what's your name?"

"None-ya," I smirked.

"None-ya?" Dhikrullah asked.

"Yeah, None-ya Business!"

In a flash, he pulled out his sword, leaped towards me, and swung it right next to my neck. He was so close to me that I could feel the adrenaline coming from his breath.

"Oh, but it is my business," he said in a hoarse whisper, "You snuck into my cave and not only stole from me, but also tried to ruin my plans for world domination. Wouldn't you say that asking your name is my business? Now listen, you little worm. I can slice your neck open without a sweat. It would be stupidly easy, like ripping a leaf in two. So, if you value your life, quit being a smart alec and answer my questions with the upmost honesty! Now let's try this again, who are you?"

I could have made a snappy remark, but I knew it would be a stupid move on my part.

"Fine," I sighed, "It's Wilhelm, King Wilhelm IV, son of King Robert V, Ruler of Rulksferd."

Immediately I heard the mob of bandits laughing their tails off, as if I said a clever joke.

"Silence!" my captor demanded, "So a king you say?"

"Don't tell me you're taking him seriously," protested a chubby thief.

"I said quite Uknamra (Uk-nam-ra)!" Dhikrullah yelled with a growl. Uknamra jumped back in response.

"So, Wilhelm IV," Dhikrullah continued, "Yes, I believe I've heard that name before. Humor me, what is the Great Mighty King Wilhelm IV doing here in the first place?"

"Thwarting your evil plan?" I replied. Yes, I know it was a lie, but it's sort of the truth as well. I had some idea what his evil plan was, and I wanted to stop it.

"Why not send your knights?" Dhikrullah remarked, "Unless you're running low on royal subjects."

"I thought it would be nice if I eradicated you guys myself," I said pretending to be brave. This brought on more laughter, even from Dhikrullah himself. Once everyone settled themselves down, Dhikrullah continued.

"Funny thing," he said before slipping in a chuckle, "Knowing tales of the royal family in Rulksferd, Robert V in particular, would have never taken such drastic actions. They'd just sit in their luxurious castles, drink their precious wine, and jest with one another, while sending their poor, overworked, and underappreciated knights to do their dirty work."

"What?" I asked astonished, "That's not true, the royal family wasn't like that all, especially my father!"

"Of course, you wouldn't know," Dhikrullah said grinding his teeth, "Because you're nothing but an imposter . . ."

He drew out his sword and rammed the butt of it into my gut.

". . . a liar . . ."

Another blow to the gut.

". . . and a thief!"

This time he stroked the butt across my cheeks.

"How much would you wager," he asked moving his sword so it could be pointed at my heart, "That the real King Wilhelm IV is in his castle right now, slave driving his servants to every simple need he could easily do himself? Now for the last time, what is your name?"

"Listen, I don't know what you have against my family," I replied, "But I am King Wilhelm IV!"

"Well," he snarled, "If you won't tell us, then I'll ask someone else. Latasha!"

"Yes, master?" a voice responded that I soon identified as the blue diamond.

"Who is this creaton that dares steal from me?" he demanded.

"His name is King Wilhelm IV," the blue emerald answered, "Just as he said with his own lips."

All the thieves gasped in shock, but Dhikrullah gave a small chuckle.

"Well, well," he said with a smirk, "Guess you weren't lying after all. Thank you."

"Your welcome?" I said bewildered by his statement.

"Yes," he remarked, "You saved me a lot of trouble. Once I had all six diamonds I was going to march towards the City of Pax, break through their walls, and show off all my power, forcing the entire valley to bow down to me. But I can show off my power right now! Uknamra!"

"Yes, sir?" he replied standing up straight.

"Begin the ceremony," Dhikrullah commanded.

"But, sir," Uknamra protested, "You said we would begin the ceremony after we celebrated."

"Well, guess what? Celebration is over, now start the ceremony!"

"Yes, sir. Right away, sir," Uknamra said with fright. He motioned himself through the crowd of thieves, while Dhikrullah followed behind him. The thieves started to establish a formation. I squirmed my body and stretched my neck as much as I could in order to see what was happening. It was either that or staring at a cave wall and just imagining what was going on.

The thieves formed lines of 9 or 10, each being perpendicular to the other. They all faced the chandelier like object. Uknamra stood in front, while Dhikrullah stood to the side. Uknamra raised the golden oil lamp rotated it a round and a round, while chanting words I could not understand. The words were mostly "ah" sounding ones with only a very few "kss" and "lils" sprinkled about. He then pointed the lamp towards the red diamond and stopped chanting. A deadly long silence followed. It was so quite you could hear a gold coin slide down one of the many piles.

*Is something supposed to be happening right now?* I wondered, assuming that this was normal for their ceremonies.

Uknamra brought the lamp back down and examined it.

"This can't be right," he stuttered. "Why isn't it working?"

"Maybe you said the wrong words this time," Dhikrullah suggested.

Uknamra preformed the whole shtick again, but the result was the same. Next, he moved the lamp differently, still nothing. He said the words slowly, he said the words quickly, he moved the lamp up and down and added words to his chant, you get the picture. Soon Uknamra was exhausted, and probably embarrassed after failing so many times.

"Why you little..." Dhikrullah said taking out his sword.

"It's the lamp!" Uknamra said trying to save his life, "It must be the wrong lamp, it must be! That little imp was on to us; he switched the lamps."

"Me?" I said offended, "I didn't do anything of the sort."

"Where is the lamp?" Dhikrullah demanded.

"I don't know," I said panicking as everyone glared at me with rage boiling from their eyes.

"Fine!" Dhikrullah asked, "I'll just ask the diamonds. Diamonds!"

"Yes, Master?" the orange emerald asked.

"Where is the lamp of the genie?" he asked.

My eyes widen. Genie? I had only heard about them in fairy tales but never thought they were actually real.

"Wait, hold up!" I yelled interrupting Esmerelda. "Those diamonds have genies inside of them, and you were about to put a genie inside the red diamond?"

"Yes, Wilhelm it is true," Esmerelda announced.

"Silence," Dhikrullah demanded, "You answer to me, and to me alone. Understand?"

"Yes, Master," Esmerelda said reluctantly.

"Answer me," he commanded, "Where is the lamp of the genie?"

"It's the one right above Wilhelm, lighting his head.

I looked up to see a golden lamp hanging on a hook connected to a wooden plank set firmly in the ground.

"What are you looking at?" Dhikrullah said to his thieves, "GET IT!"

The thieves stumbled in a mad dash, the side effects from all the alcohol showed their toll.

With all my strength, I forced the chair to fall backward against the wooden pole. It shook but not enough to release the golden lamp. I wiggled the chair this way and that, trying to shake the lamp off its hook. The thieves were getting closer. Dhikrullah could have gotten through if his thieves weren't so smooshed together on all sides.

They were only inches away from me. I had to make my last attempt count. With every bone in my body I shook the chair with all my might. The lamp fell off the hook and down onto my lamp. I gave it a good rub with my neck, and the lamp burst with life.

Streams of fire whizzed out of opening; red smoke poured out like a river. A small groan could be heard from the lamp. It got louder, and louder, and louder. A paw with claws popped out, then an arm, then a head with pointy ears, then a body, and finally the other hand. Yes, sir, I had my very own genie and she was strange as she was beautiful.

"OYE!" she proclaimed, "About time someone released me from my..."

She looked around. Everyone, including me, was frozen in shock. We must have made one crazy looking bunch.

"Oh, excuse me, I've come at a wrong time," she said, "I'm going to go back in my lamp now, okay?"

"No, wait!" I exclaimed, "I wish you could beat these guys up!"

"You're wish is my command sir!" said the genie forming to attention. She fought every single thief in the cavern to a bloody pulp. She threw a few punches at some, and smashed heavy objects on to others. It was by far the most violent thing I had ever seen in my entire life.

She came towards Dhikrullah and whacked him with a long and thick wooden stick. Where'd she get it from? I don't know, probably poofed it into existence or whatnot.

I leaned the chair forward, which resulted in me falling to the ground with a thud. I motioned towards one of the bodies and drew out their sword. With careful precision I was able to cut the ropes and free myself.

I looked up to see only one thief standing. The genie rushed towards him, until he decided to knock himself out with his own fist. With that, the genie gave a victorious smirk.

"Alright genie," I replied recovering the lamp, "I wish we were far away from this place, as far as we can be."

"Wait," I heard Latasha say, "What about us?"

*Oh, crap!* I realized that I forgot to mention the other genies trapped in the diamonds in my wish.

"When I say we, I mean..." I began to clarify, but the genie was already working her magic.

I felt myself disappearing. I raced towards the chandelier hoping to grab one of the emeralds. I had my paw on one, when everything in the cave faded from a few.

"No," I cried, "Not like this, not like this!"

I blinked only for a second and *boom!* I saw the vast blue ocean waves come in and out with the tide. I heard the sound of seagulls flying from afar. I felt the warm sandy beach sinking into my paws. The sight of the sun was blocked by some leaves from above. I was on an island, in the middle of nowhere, with a genie, a lamp and nothing else.

# CHAPTER V

You've probably figured out by now; I had made a lot of mistakes during my short life. Heck, me being a king of an entire country was a mistake on its own merit. Anyway, the point is, I never realized the weight of my mistakes. If I had messed up before, at least the entire world wouldn't be in danger.

But, when I made the mistake of not bring the diamonds with me, I couldn't let it down. I had the chance to be the hero, a real chance to make up my wrongs, and now that chance was gone, forever.

I kicked the sand in frustration and screamed at the tide every time it came near me.

"Someone's angry," I heard the genie say from behind me. I turned myself around, facing her.

"You would be too. If you just let me finish my wish I could have been a hero!" I yelled.

"Well, you would be angry if you granted someone's wish and they're upset with you, like it was your fault," snapped the genie, "What? Why are you looking at me like that?"

"Nothing," I replied staring at her, "I just never imagined a genie would act like you."

"Hey, I'm a critter too," the genie quipped, "Or was, but that was a long time ago."

There was nothing else I felt like I could say to her. I wanted to kick the sand some more, but I wasn't angry enough to, so I began to walk towards where all the plants were growing.

"You know," the genie said following me, "You could just wish to make it all better."

"No thanks," I replied, "I want to save my last wish for an absolute emergency."

I heard the genie give a displeasing grunt in defeat.

"So, what are you going to do now?" the genie asked.

"I'm going to build a raft," I told her, "With plenty of trees and leaves, what more could an animal ask for?"

I found a pretty tall tree with a trunk that was about the size of my head.

"What are you going to do, chop it down with your teeth?" the genie gave a snarky laugh. I knew what she was doing, a clever plan, but it wasn't going to work on me. However, she had a good point, try as I might I could never have brought down that tree without an ax.

*Maybe I don't need a tree* I thought to myself. I imagined my raft being held together with twigs and leaves. With ambition in paw, I collected all the twigs and leaves I could find and brought them back to the shore line.

The genie chuckled, as she watched me fail multiple times trying to get two twigs to connect together.

"How about you go back into your lamp and stay there?" I asked.

"And miss out on this?" she asked, "No way!"

I continued to work on the raft, and despite the genie watching in spite, it eventually looked like a raft. The dumb genie couldn't bring this lemming down. Even the winds were on my side. For a tropical island, it sure got cold pretty quickly, then it got freezing cold, then it became so cold I knew something was up. The wind was blowing so hard the trees looked like they were about to be rooted out of the ground.

Dark, grey, clouds came sailing across the sky. Bolts of lightning were greeted by dreadful rumbles of thunder, which shook the ground. I had to find shelter and fast.

I ran as quickly as I could and dove right into the jungle. I began to search for a cave, a mountain range, or at least two rocks acting like walls supporting a big giant rock as a roof. But I was not so lucky, for there were only trees and shrubbery as far I could see. The storm came sooner than I expected. The rain made the uneven ground unbearably slippery.

The only type of "shelter" I could find was two plants with giant leaves. As far as shelters went this one was pretty pathetic.

"You know," said genie startling me with her presence, "You could just wish for a shelter and you could be nice and dry right now."

"How did you get here?" I asked bewildered, "And besides I know what you're up to, and it won't work!"

"First, there are no rules saying a genie can't hold her own lamp," she answered, "Secondly, what do you think I'm up to?"

"Isn't it obvious?" I cried out. "You want me to waste my last wish so you can go back into that tin can of yours and not be bothered again."

"Are you kidding me?" she said with a stern look on her face, "Believe me, the last thing I want is to be in that 'tin can' as you called it."

"Then why are you tempting me?" I asked her. The thunder started to roar constantly, rain was pouring down by the boat load.

"I just want to see when you'll start to crack," she explained.

"Is that all?" I said practically screaming to the top of my lungs.

"Hey, don't blame me that I've been locked and bored to tears," she continued, "A genie has to have some fun."

I was about to make a quick remark, but then I felt a painful ache in my stomach as it began to make a gurgling sound.

"Sounds like somebody's hungry," the genie said teasingly, "Just one wish could make it all better."

"No thank-you genie," I replied harshly, but she was right I was getting terribly hungry. All my mind could think about was food. My mind went back to the life I had in the palace; giant roasted chicken dinner, surrounded by grapes and apples, with luscious corn-on-the-cob and steamy potatoes on the side. I remembered the warmth of the flames coming from the ginormous furnace smack dab in the middle of the dining room. Oh, I could just wish to go back to those days. But no, I was determined to not make a wish unless I really needed one.

I looked on the ground below me to see insects of every shape, color, and size crawl around my paws. They might have been gross, living, and unsanitary beings, but they were the only source of food I had. True, I could have eaten the leaves of my "shelter", but the leaves didn't seem so nutritious to me.

"Gross," said the genie in disgust, "You're not seriously going to eat those bugs, are you?"

As if to say "you bet", I picked up a small beetle with a purple head and pink shell over its body.

"Ewwww," the genie said in disgust, "I can't watch."

The bug crawled around my hands, just as I was putting it inside my mouth. I bit down hard, only to realize that the bug was scurrying around my teeth.

*Maybe I should have killed it first* I thought to myself, but at that moment it didn't really matter. It was already taking residency in my mouth and there was no going back. I opened my mouth wide and waited for the little guy to crawl on top of my bottom teeth. I bit down hard.

At first impact, it felt like eating a walnut, but as my teeth applied more pressure it felt like I was eating a grape. The taste was extremely off the wall; I can't seem to find a good way to describe it. It had a meaty type of flavor to it, with a touch of blueberry.

After chewing two or four more times, I finally swallowed, and I showed the genie my teeth so she could see there was nothing to it. My gloating was short lived when I felt six legs crawl up my throat and back onto my tongue. I swallowed it a third time, but the same thing happened. It must have been quite a sight for the genie when I opened my mouth to reveal the beetle resting on my tongue. Although the rain was coming in harsh, I could hear her making a fake barfing noise that I've heard little kids do when they're disgusted.

I moved my tonnage forward so the bug would be right under my teeth. I bit down hard, and a sharp pain drove me to tears. The beetle was smarter than I thought. My short scream of pain, allowed it the chance to jump off my tongue and land back on the ground without a scratch.

The genie gave a laugh at my expense, right before I hit the bug with my paw so it wouldn't escape again. I picked it up and ate the beetle once again, this time it went down all the way with one large gulp.

My stomach was still unsatisfied, so I looked below to see what other insects were still crawling around. I saw what looked like a big thick centipede or a millipede – didn't matter to me at the time – slithering this way and that. I stepped on what I deduced was its stomach and I picked it up.

"Are you crazy?" I heard the genie shout in fright, "Don't eat that..."

But I didn't let her finish. In complete ignorance, I tossed the little guy into my mouth and ate in pride.

"Millipedes are poisonous, don't you know that?" I heard her say at the top of her lungs. My eyes widened. Right then I regretted everything I had ever done. But wait, how was I supposed to know she wasn't pulling my leg or something. True, it did have a bitter after taste. True, it did burn down my neck like strong wine, but none of that meant it was poison. But unlike strong wine, the burning sensation of my throat got worse, as if it suddenly caught on fire! I couldn't get the strong after taste off my tongue. My heart began to beat at a rapid pace. The world began to move, as if I was standing underwater. The sounds of raindrops, harsh winds, and crackling thunder all seemed to fade.

Suddenly, I felt like a creature had forced itself down inside of me. The impact felt like more of an implosion, as if whatever hit me became a part of me. My insides became warmer and warmer, but it wasn't the painful type burn from the poison, more like a warm toasty burning sensation. I felt like I was going to gag. I involuntarily shoved my head down to the ground and started puking. I vomited out an orange paw with pointed claws, like the paw and claws my genie had. The paw held out the millipede and placed it on the ground. By gratuitous force, my body sucked the paw back in, and whatever collided with my body came straight out, and the warm sensation was gone.

I coughed a few times to get a hold of myself. It was then when I realized, the after taste was finally gone, my heart slowed down, sounds around me became crystal clear, and everything around me became stable as it was before.

I looked at the genie with amazement.

"You're welcome," she said with a smirk, "If you don't mind I'll go back in my 'tin can' now, let me know if you do anything stupid."

Red smoke sucked back into the golden lamp, leaving me bewildered with more questions than answers. As the storm worsened and as I found more bugs to eat, I had a desperate desire to show my sincere gratitude towards the genie.

# CHAPTER VI

The next day came, and the storm finally faded away. I was able to find a little waterfall deeper within the jungle. I used it to bathe and rehydrate myself when the occasion arose.

Throughout this day, I could never take my mind off of finding some way to thank the genie for saving my life. There was no point in making her something unless it could fit inside her little bottle.

In the meantime, I was finally able to make a tiny shelter with just rods of wood and long strands of shrubbery. It took me quiet a while to figure out how to get the pieces to stand upright. The wind wasn't any help, either knocking it over or scattering towards the beach. I was beyond happy when I finally figured it out. The little hut I had made struct was triangular, with a big opening. Probably not one of the sturdiest structures in the world, but if it could withstand the winds then it was good enough for me.

As the sun began to set in the horizon, I thought I might as well start a fire. I went off of information I heard around the castle, about people starting a fire by just rubbing sticks against a rock. I gathered a bunch of sticks, placed them down on the ground, found a stone, picked up one stick, and rubbed the stone against it as hard as I could.

Nothing happened. I did it again. Zilch. I did it faster this time. Not even a sign of a spark. I scratched that stick so hard and for so long, the end was pointy enough to be a knife.

Suddenly red smoke came out of the lamp, and the genie appeared.

"Hold up," she said, "My Stupid Alarm went off. Let's see, trying to start a fire, eh? Ah, I see the problem."

She whizzed away within a matter of seconds, but she came back just as fast.

"Here ya go," she said tossing a hairy mess into my paws, "Here's an easier way to start a fire, you rub these two rods against each other, keep doing it until you see smoke and charred wood dust coming out, dump the charred dust into the coconut husk I gave you, give the dust a good pinch, blow and place it over the pile. Oh, it'd be best to draw a circle around the sticks, and lay the stone on the borders, okay?"

"Yeah, no prob," I said amazed.

She turned around to see my wimpy, raged excuse for a shelter.

"Cute shelter," she said, "Not a winner for best building of the year, but it will do."

"Nothing to it," I said with confidence.

"Well, I'll see ya," she said going back into her lamp.

"Wait," I said stopping her, "Before you go, I don't believe we've been properly introduced. My name's Wilhelm IV."

I held out my paw, waiting for a response. She hesitated for a second, but then floated towards me. Her face looked like she wanted to say something but couldn't let it out.

"What is it?" I asked concerned.

"Well to be honest you can give me a name if you'd like," she answered.

"What would you want to be called?" I asked.

"Well if that's the case," she said with a grin, "My old master called me slave, but from now on I would like to be called Helina."

"Helina it is," I replied.

"Well how do you Sir Wilhelm IV," she said doing a little curtsy and shaking my paw, "My name is, Helina, daughter of Gerstiflied the fruit seller."

Once we let go of each other's paws, we both seemed to chuckle in unison.

"I beg your pardon Miss Helina," I said with a pretend snooty tone, "But, I don't believe I've seen an animal like you before. What are you?"

"Well, Sir Wilhelm IV," she said playfully, "I am a lynx. Sort of like a bob cat, except we have pointy ears and all that rough."

"Well I'll see you later, Helina," I said happily.

"Will do," she replied heading back to her lamp, "Until your next immediate blunder."

The red smoke appeared again, taking her back into her precious lamp. If the pressure wasn't on to show my gratitude before, it was on that very moment. As I rubbed the two sticks together, just as she told me, an idea formed in my mind. I figured that I could write her a sonnet. Where I came from, creatures wrote sonnets all the time to express their imagination, affection, and appreciation.

With a fire going, I went right to work. Since, I didn't have any paper I just wrote what I was going to say right there in the sand. Finding the right words was easier said than done. This was extremely harder than setting the fire or building the shelter. Once I finally thought I had a breakthrough, the fire would start to dim and I would have to search for more twigs. By the time I placed them on the pile, the words either escaped my memory or they proved ineffective for fitting my emotions.

I slaved all through the night. It was quite an ordeal, but I finally I finished it. I would have kissed my paw-etched words in the sand, but they would have been all smudge up and unreadable.

With the whole thing committed to memory, I chose to recite it for Helina right before noon. Pleased over a good day's work, I walked into my shelter and laid down on the floor.

I realized that being caught up in making the fire and the sonnet made me forget to make some sort of bedding. I got back up again and meandered towards the jungle. I found two big leaves that had fallen off from one of the palm trees, walked back to shelter, placed them on the ground one next to the other, and finally I laid myself down on top of them.

I did my best to wonder off into dream land, but I started hearing these strange noises coming from the jungle. They were very high pitched, almost like they were made by children. But soon I was able to shrug it off, and I fell into a deep slumber.

***

My mind sprung to life, and I slowly lifted up my head and realized that my bladder was screaming that it was filled to the max. My joints were as stiff as wood, if I so dared move even my tiniest muscle, I was greeted by a blast of unforgivable suffering. I trotted to the edge of the jungle, pulled down my underwear and let it all go.

Once receiving a succession thank-you from my bladder, my stomach started complaining. Two options for breakfast were; insects or fruit. Insects were easy to find, while fruit was harder; however, I had never had tropical fruit before. With my mind made up, I searched for any fruit I could find. Within minutes of searching in the jungle, I found two bushes; one with blue berries the other with red berries. The question was which one was poisonous and which one was not. I decided not to risk it, so I moved on.

I found a tall banana tree with rippend produce waiting to be devoured. It was pretty skinny to be considered a tree, and I was curious how the thing didn't bend over from all the weight. I tried kicking it, but my joints would torture me.

"Come on Wilhelm," I said stretching my legs, "You can do this."

I forced each kick to the tree, no matter how much misery my legs put me through. With one final kick, the banana tree came crashing down with a thud. It was time to reap the harvest.

Ripping out the entire batch of bananas proved futile. I coughed up some spit onto my paws, rubbed them against each other, and, with all my strength, I pulled one of the bananas. The banana came out like a sword from a stone, and once I finally had one in my paws, why not get two or three more for the road?

I was on my way to the shelter, when I realized that I needed to brush myself up if I were to appear my best in front of Helina. After throwing the last of my bananas on to the rough terrain, I splashed my face with clean and pure water.

With a spring in my step I headed back to my shelter. My paws stopped at Helina's golden lamp. In my mind, I went through the entire sonnet making sure I remembered everything to the letter.

I was about to announce my presence, when the red smoke beat me to it.

"Alright," Helina said squeezing out of the lamp, "Let's get this over with."

"You know what I'm going to do?" I asked disappointed, I was really hoping for this to be a surprise.

"No," she said, and I gave a sigh of relief. "It's just that my Stupid Alarm went off, so you're about to do something stupid. So, let's get it over with. What are you about to do?"

I ignored what she said and went straight into reciting my sonnet.

*"Oh Helina, I had no idea that when I met you,*

*You would ..."*

"Wait, hold up," she interrupted.

"What?" I asked confused, "I know it's kind of sappy but..."

"Let me finish," she said calmly, she took a deep breath and said, "Listen, Wilhelm. I'm flattered really, but you don't have to do this for me."

"But I want to," I protested, "I need to. You don't understand, throughout my life I haven't known a single soul who would actually save my life."

"Don't be melodramatic," she said scoffing at the idea, "You probably know some animals who would protect you against all odds."

"Well, true, I did," I replied, "But they're gone now. Anyway, as I was saying, I lead my entire life as a selfish and arrogant brat who thought too much of himself to make friends or to rule a kingdom. Everyone hated me, and rightfully so. My own advisors turned on me, and the rest is history. Serves me right."

Helina held her head low unable to respond.

"But you, you're different," I said holding my tears back. "You saved my life, even though I was being a pompous jerk to you. You could have let me die by my own paws, and I wouldn't blame you if you did. I would have let myself die too. But instead, you cared about me so much that that you didn't leave me to death's door..."

I had to catch my breath. The most agonizing part was waiting for Helina to say something. Her face was mournful, as if she had witnessed a horrible death. Suddenly, she let out a sigh and began to speak.

"Wilhelm," she started with much difficulty, "The reason I saved you was because I am your genie, and being your genie, I'm bound by force to protect you."

So, that was why she saved me.

"I know that sounds bad but hear me out. Before I was a genie, I lived my life as the happy daughter of a fruit seller. Life was simple back then I met this one weasel, his name was Kharull (Ka-rule) Zalshi (Zal-shee)."

She stopped as if she was pondering whether to continue.

"Me and him were quite an item back in the day," she said, "He flattered me. He gave me things that I didn't even want, but his gifts were so beautiful and seemed sincere I accepted them anyway. But, one fateful day, he told me to meet him near a specific cave and to not tell my parents where I had gone. Being as naïve as I was, I complied and waited for him to arrive."

She gave a little scoff.

"I should have known better," she said with rage taking shape on her face, "That sneaky weasel with great haste, rubbed an empty genie lamp against my body. Before I could ask him what he was doing, my body began to tingle. I blinked for a moment, and suddenly I felt power shoving itself into my veins. Power to grant wishes, power to control space and time itself. It was liberating at first, but the moment was short lived when a red vortex of smoke and ash sucked me into the golden lamp.

Kharull made a cackling laugh.

'You're mine now slave,' he said.

It was then I realized that he didn't love me. He just wanted some eye candy to give him unimaginable power and to serve him at his beckoning call. He rubbed the lamp and I became his personal slave. He wished for his cave to be filled with treasure, and I granted it. He went into my home village one day, and wished for everyone to worship him, and I had no choice but to comply. I didn't want the people I loved to become his slaves, it was horrifying to see my family become mindless zombies for him, but what could I do? I had no power to interfere with his sick and malicious plans.

He made all the males his thieves. If the females were young, he would make them part of his harem. If the females were old, they would cook him food and take care of the other males.

The most horrendous part was when he and his men went out to raid other villages, he was protected by yours truly. I hated covering for him.

He ordered me out of my lamp one day and commanded me to wear this degrading outfit you see me in now. It was then when I had it. I made sure he had a piece of my mind. We argued for a strenuous amount of time, until he ended the argument by saying:

'I wish that I never knew you!'

And poof! I was back in my lamp, and he had no idea what he had done to deserve such a following or such wealth. Probably thought that was how his life had always been. Soon he died. With his death I assumed his followers snapped out of their trance, but I'm not quite sure. I didn't care either way because I was happy in my little lamp, wishing to never be someone's genie ever again."

I didn't know what to say, I didn't even know if it would be wise to say anything at all. I felt like I needed to respond in some way, but I didn't know how. Helina was in so much distress, and there I was, helplessly staring at her.

"But you know what," she said regaining her strength, "When I was forced to save you, I felt a joy in my heart that I never felt for such a long time. You know why? Because unlike Kharull, you actually treated me as a living being, not as an object, but as a decent creature. When I saved you, I felt like I somehow saved the world."

"What do you mean?" I asked, "I treated you like crap."

I did not mean to upset Helina even further, but it was the truth. I was a coward, a liar, and a brat, nothing good could come out of me.

"Oh, come off it," she said annoyed, "Do you think Kharull showed any gratitude towards me, in the form of a sonnet no less? You're not like him, Wilhelm. Yes, you treated me like crap, yes you might have done terrible things in the past, but you know what?"

"What?" I asked.

"I know for a fact, you want to change," she said hitting the nail on the coffin, "Kharull never wanted that. You don't want to be a despicable animal any more. So, I don't need any other form of gratitude because of it."

Helina was right. Now that I thought about it, what good was a sonnet anyhow? It was just an assortment of flattering words, anyone could do that. I needed something that would put those words into action.

"Listen, Helina," I said suddenly, "I promise to you with all my heart, that I will no longer be the selfish, arrogant, fearful, wretched lemming that I was, and I will use this second chance to be a kind, thoughtful, wise, brave, honorable lemming that I need to be."

Helina floated closer to me than she ever had before, and gently gave a small kiss on my cheek.

"I'd like that very much," she said pleased. The promise was not a string of words, but words that I would indeed act upon. No power was going to stand in between me and my word.

# CHaPTER Vii

Falling asleep on the island proved more and more difficult. For seven continuous night I heard children's screams in the distance, it was on night number eight when I was rudely awaken from my slumber.

"WILHELM!" I heard Helina.

I jumped up in a blind panic only to realize I was no longer in my shelter. I was lying on the rough beach with a net underneath me.

"What's going on?" I asked looking this way and that. I saw small flames scattered across the beach.

*That's funny* I thought to myself *I thought I put out the fire before I went to bed.*

I noticed lying next to the flames, kids, covered with fig leaves and mud specifically placed on their bodies and faces. They were all groaning in s pain, as if they had the daylights knocked out of 'em. Helina floated in the middle, with her back straight and proud.

"What's going on here?" I asked confused.

"I caught these little guys trying to kidnap you!" she announced, "Luckily I caught them just in time. Now what were you little critters up to?"

"We needed him for a sacrifice," a pudgy hedgehog said while uncurling himself.

"Sacrifice?" I said disturbed, "A sacrifice for what?"

"To our god," a thin squirrel said, failing to pull himself up.

"Every full moon, The Great Mighty Boar demands our loyalty in a form of a sacrifice," a chipmunk explained. "If we don't, he'll kill us all!"

Helina and I looked at each other with bewilderment. A 'Great Mighty Boar', where did that come from?

"Where are your parents?" I asked them.

"We don't know," the thin squirrel replied. "We were sent to fight in the war. Our ship was attacked by pirates. We were the only ones to survive the ordeal, and we swam to this island. At first life without adults around seemed like fun, but then chaos ensued as we all wanted to do things our own way. It all stopped when the Great Mighty Boar came and brought order back into our lives."

I started feeling sorry for the little kids, but I had to get to the bottom of this.

"He then started to want sacrifices," the hedgehog continued, "At first, he sounded reasonable, only requesting fruits and vegetables. It was like this for a month or two, until one day he wanted us to sacrifice one of our own. We didn't want to do it, but he got all mad and threatened to eat us all whole. We didn't know what to do, but when we saw you, we knew you had to be our sacrifice."

The hedgehog took a few deep breaths, trying to get on his own two paws again.

On one paw the idea of a *Giant Boar* like god out for blood sounded preposterous to me. However, the fear on each of the children's faces were real. So, if there wasn't a Giant Boar out there, then what were they afraid of?

"Listen," I said taking it all in, "I don't know of this *Great Mighty Boar* you guys speak of, but there has to be another way other than blood sacrifice."

"But if we don't then he'll squish us all," a bunny called out.

"Well we'll kill him then," I said confidently.

"How?" asked a porcupine, "His skin is as tough as iron, his teeth can bite through rock, and his feet are as big as castles."

"Well we'll just have to think of..." I was about to say when the ground began to shake. A loud booming voice could be heard singing:

> *"Oh, where oh where is my sacrifice?*
> *Oh, why isn't there?*
> *If I can't have my sacrifice,*
> *You boys better beware!"*

The kids started to run in a panic, doing their best to hide. A possum faked his own death, the rabbit hid behind a rock and the squirrel climbed up a tree.

"Did I mention he loves to sing?" the hedgehog asked before forming himself into a ball.

The ground started to shake more violently with each step.

"Ready to take down a god?" Helina asked.

"Honestly," I said with a gulp, "I don't know."

Suddenly, I saw it, and boy was he huge! The mere sight of him turned my fur white. His skin was a fiery red, his eyes were bright yellow, and his hair was dark black. His tusks were about the size of the palm trees, and his nose was the size of a boulder. His voice blew the leaves off the trees, and its breath rotted everything in its path

It looked at me and Helina, before belching into song.

> *"Why hello there, my little prey.*
> *It's safe to say, it's your final day.*
> *Prepare to be no-more,*
> *For I am the Great Mighty Boar!"*

"Any idea how to stop him?" Helina asked as the monster raised its ginormous feet above the trees.

"Ummm... let me think about it!" I screamed running for my life.

"You better find out soon," Helina warned, as the boar crashed its foot down to an earthshaking thud, "You're running out of island."

The creature sang again.

> *"Your bones will be crushed to nothing.*
> *Your guts I will be munching.*
> *I take pride in eating gore,*
> *For I am the Great Mighty Boar!"*

*Oh rats!* I thought to myself. I was knee deep down in the murky ocean water, with no idea on how to kill this beast.

"Hey Helina," I screamed. "Are you able to fight this thing?"

"Only one way to find out," she said before rocketing off towards the monster. She flung her fists, she scratched with her claws, she took a big bite out of his skin, but to our shock, nothing seemed to leave a mark. The boar gave out a laugh and sang;

> *"What is this now? Oh, can it be?*
> *You send a genie to fight me?*
> *I do not have one single sore,*
> *For I am the Great Mighty Boar!"*

How did he know she was genie? Had he'd seen one before? Why weren't any of her attacks working? Those questions were left unanswered as my brain was rushing with panic. "Since attacking it head on won't work," I said thinking aloud, "Then there must be some other way."

I then had a terrible idea, so juvenile and stupid, that it just might just fail. Yet, it was the only one I had.

"Hey pork breath!" I shouted getting the boar's attention, "Sing another line for me."

The boar took a deep breath and sang a verse.

> *"I've never heard such a request,*
> *Surely my prey you must je..."*

"Rest?" I interrupted, "Well I wanted to, but then you just wanted your sacrifice."

It began to growl.

> *"Listen you, you little shmuck,*
> *It's not polite to inter..."*

"Erupt?" I asked, "I don't know, looks like you're going to erupt any second now."

"Wilhelm you're just making him madder," Helina cautioned.

"Don't worry," I reassured, "I just have to figure out how to use this to my advantage."

I took a brief inventory of my surroundings. Since I was closer to the ocean, I thought of leading it to drown, but I would have drowned before the boar ever had a chance. I then looked at Helina, eying me with a worried look. I remembered her story, and how she became a genie in the first place.

"Hey kids!" I shouted attempting to jumpstart my plan, "Distract him for me will ya?"

> *"What an incredibly stupid tactic
> I'll let you know I'm not easily..."*

"Fantastic?" the squirrel interrupted, "You don't say."

*Good* I thought *Now for phase two of my plan.*

"Helina," I announced to her.

"Yeah?" she asked.

"I'm ready for my final wish," I replied.

"Well, let's hear it," she said reluctantly

"Helina," I said, "I wish that you were free!"

Helina's eyes widen. She was about to say something when her lamp started to violently shake. A spark of energy formed between Helina and the lamp, getting bigger and bigger, before shrinking in size, and blowing up in a bright explosion.

The light faded away, and I saw Helina standing on her own two paws in front of me.

"Oh Wilhelm!" she exclaimed, as she floated towards me to give me a hug, but something stopped her. It was like an invisible force was holding her back. She took one step in front of the other, trying to push back against it, but the force was so strong it knocked her off her paws and pulled her across the sandy beach like a ragdoll. She tried to grab a hold of anything in sight, but her paws phased through it all.

"WILHELM!" she shouted in fright.

"Helina!" I shouted helplessly.

Helina gave out another scream, before she was sucked into the clouds above.

She was gone, with only the golden lamp to her name.

"Sir Wilhelm!" I heard one of the boys shout. I wanted all time to stop right then and there. I needed time to take it all in, but that would have to wait.

I turned back to face the giant boar once again. I ran towards it, grabbing Helina's lamp on the way. I rushed with all my might while giving the first battle cry I had ever given.

The boar was about to sing a second verse, but I wasn't going to let him finish. I rubbed the lamp against his skin, and let the magic happen.

Sparks flew from the lamp. A giant vortex spewed from the opening. The vortex became stronger and stronger, forcing clouds in the sky to form a spiral tunnel above the boar. The winds were so strong, even the sand from the beach was sucked into the lamp.

"What's going on?" the boar asked, "No, no!"

It was sickening for me to watch his muscles and bones becoming distorted and liquidity. The vortex continued to squeeze the boar's body into itself.

"Oh, what a world, what a world!" the boar exclaimed in pain, "Who knew a bunch of good woodland creatures like you could bring an end to my godliness!"

The body was now sucked in, leaving his head the only thing untouched.

"I'm going!" the boar said afraid, "I'm gone! I'm...ooooooohhhhhhh!"

A burst of wind sent the clouds back in to the sky, and the golden lamp fell with a satisfactory thud, and the sand fell like rain on to the ground.

The boys were in a state of shock for a second or two. It wasn't long before they started celebrating with victorious shouts. I wanted to join them, but I couldn't bring myself to do it. I looked up into the sky, where I last saw Helina.

I tried mustering the strength to say something, but my tears choked me before I could say it.

"Thank you, Helina," I finally managed to say. "Thank you."

# CHAPTER VIII

The ninth day barely began, and I was completely drained of all my physical and emotional strength. All I could think about was how Helina was torn away from me. I left the boys in their celebration and walked into what was left of the forest. There was so much I wanted to express yet had little strength to do it. Whether I was griping in my mind or talking out loud, I had no clue. The fact still remained that Helina was gone, and there was nothing I could do but hope she was in better place than here.

My mind became foggy. I soon found myself lying on crumbled leaves, closing my eyes in exhaustion. Within a snap, daylight flooded my vision. The kids were looking down at me with concerned looks on their faces.

"Sir?" the hedgehog asked worryingly, "Are you okay?"

"I'm good," I replied half awake. The hard surface proved not too friendly for my already stiff back.

"What do we do now?" asked a younger squirrel.

The jungle was now just a big graveyard of trees, with bruised fruit scattered throughout.

"For a start," I replied, "How about we build ourselves a boat? There's nothing for us here now."

This caused a joyful reaction from the kids.

"But wait," the hedgehog exclaimed bringing a halt to the celebration, "We don't know how to build a boat. If we did, we would have left weeks ago."

The little guy did have a point there.

"I guess there's no better time to learn than right now. "I remarked, and with that we set to work.

\*\*\*

"Alright guys!" I shouted, "Let's see what this gal is made of. One... two...three!"

In unison we pushed our boat onto the blue waters. Our boat had at least ten or twenty modifications attached to it, but the boys and I had hoped our hard work would pay off.

Through the endless modifications, I was able to spend time getting to know them. It was quite a challenge to get all the names down. Their names were; Timmore (the squirrel) son of Jacob, Berry (the hedgehog) the son Vicesimal, his brothers (oldest to youngest) Marcus, Nathanial and Gregory, one rabbit named Gurbert and another one named Smee both sons of Cush, another rabbit named Marvell son of Ruppert, Cravon (the porcupine) son of James, Joseph (the possum) son of Yidd and his two twin brothers Samuel I and Samuel II, and finally two badgers Michal son of Hagi and Robert son of Calve.

I learned that Timmore had declared himself the leader before the Great Mighty Boar took over, so I had him as my second in command. Berry was the smartest one out of the bunch, so I had him as an advisor. I assigned Michal and Samuel II to help find food and firewood. I put those three in charge of getting supplies for the boat and whatever foods they could scavenge from the debris. Samuel I and Cravon had built the huts, which were crushed by the boar, so I put them in charge of organizing the other kids into building the boat.

Full discloser, I did not choose to be the leader of the group. It was just decided that since I was the only adult, I had the final word in everything. We had a few kinks, like some of the kids understandably complained that we were never going to get off this island, but other than that our team was an unstoppable machine.

Once the boat hit the water, we were all relieved that it had passed the floating test, it was then time to see if it could pass the weight test.

"Okay everyone," I announced, "Let's bring it back in."

Samuel II trudged in the water around the boat to push the front end, while Robert went to the back end to pull it forward. When the boat hit the surface of the beach, we took some of the heaviest rocks on the island and placed them on to the boat. Then we sent it back to sea. For a moment, it almost looked like the boat wouldn't be able to make it, but we were relieved to see all of our hard work had finally paid off.

As Samuel II and Robert brought in the boat one final time, the boys began to shout with glee.

"Hold on," I said bring the merriment to a halt. "We still have some more work to do."

All the boys groaned, before gathering around me to get further instructions. I was no expert in ship building by any means, but from what I had seen in illustrations and heard from stories, I knew we needed some way of controlling it.

"First," I said to the group, "We need to make some oars, and finally we'll need an anchor."

"Aye, aye, sir!" the kids replied. Berry, Samuel II, and Cravon put their heads together. It wasn't long until they had 14 oars ready for use. The oar was made of flat pieces from tree bark attached to a wooden rod by tying it with thick grass.

Next up was constructing the anchor. We got the biggest boulder from the pile as the anchor, and some of the boys offered their tattered shirts for the rope. We tied the line of shirts around the rock, before tying it to the edge of the ship.

"Good job boys," I said brushing the sweat off my forehead, "Looks like we have a ship that is seaworthy."

The boys began to jump around and yelling "Yeah!" or "We did it!" I celebrated with them in my head, for I was completely exhausted.

"Can we sail now?" the kids asked gathering around me.

"Let's rest until tomorrow," I suggested. Hearing disappoint from the rest of the group, I added, "But, that doesn't mean we can't have a little party!"

The boys cheered in unison.

"Go on," I encouraged, "Enjoy yourself, you guys deserve it!"

The boys didn't need me to tell them twice. They played all sorts of games that me and my brothers and I used to play. They even persuaded me to play along with them. We ate from the food supplies, and Timmore showed me how to make water drinkable by boiling it. He filled his water jug with sea water and placed it over the fire until it boiled. The water became drinkable once he moved it away from the fire and allowed it to cool down for a minute or two.

The sun was setting when we finished building our little boat, and by the time we were celebrating the moon was already above the horizon. The boys made a fire all by themselves, and we passed the time away by telling and singing stories.

"Hey, Sir Wilhelm," Timmore shouted, "Tell us a story."

Despite my hesitation, the request turned into a big group chant.

"Alright, alright," I said chuckling, "Maybe one story."

The only story I could think of at the time was my own. Yet the boys were looking up to me as a hero, and if I did tell them the truth, they would see what a despicable creature I was. Then it hit me.

"Okay I got a good one," I announced, "It's called The Selfish King... Jeffory... yeah Jeffory."

I told them how *Jeffory* didn't want to be king, so he started making made up laws that drove everyone to hate him. One day they kicked *Jeffory* off the throne, and he was sent wondering the desert.

"Soon he found a cave," I said continuing Jeffory's story, the boys were at the edge of their seats, "He saw that the cave was filled with riches and treasures in the whole world. To his horror, he found out that the entrance to the cave had been sealed, and there was no way for him to escape. So, he lived in the cave alone for the rest of his days. The End."

I looked around. Some of the younger boys - Nathanial, Gregory, Smee, and Robert - looked like they were about to cry, while the older boys looked confused.

"What happened to the people in his kingdom?" asked Berry.

"They started their own government, and they were fine," I answered.

"Who came up with their government?" Berry asked.

"I don't know, maybe Jeffory's advisors," I replied.

"How did they know they'd chose the right one?" Cravon asked.

"I don't know."

"Did Jeffory really die in the cave?" asked Gregory worriedly.

"Who found all the treasure before Jeffory?" Berry asked

"Why couldn't he get out?" Nathanael asked.

"Which government did they choose?" pondered Cravon.

"Hold it!" Timmore announced silencing the group. "Maybe Wilhelm needs to sleep on it. It is a story after all."

"Yeah," I said in a way relieved.

***

The night passed on. While the boys slept with ease, I could not. My mind was troubled by the state I had left Rulksferd in. Who knew how many lives were lost, buildings destroyed, crops burned, families broken in the face of such chaos. They had Rudding and my other former advisors, but because of their betrayal, I questioned what they were up to. To add more troubles on to my back, Dhikrullah and his merry gang of thieves were off trying to conquer the world with genie magic, as well as seeking revenge upon my head. To top it all off, I had a whole troop of boys to look after, with each of them looking up to me.

I was just as helpless and afraid as I was back home. One part of me wanted to run away and ditch the kids, but I quietly told myself:

"No! Shut up, that's stupid. That's something the old Wilhelm would do; you're not him anymore."

I just couldn't take it and decided that the best thing for me to do, was to take a nice walk. Maybe after walking around the island I would finally be tired enough to put all my thoughts to rest.

It was a beautiful night. The waves rhythmically moved up and down the coast, while the crickets were now brave enough to sing their songs. To me it felt like nature itself was singing me its own lullaby.

"Hoi, Sir Wilhelm," I heard a voice shout. I jumped, only to see Timmore hanging from a tree right beside me.

"You're a sneaky little one," I said, looking up at him.

"Thanks," Timmore chipped up before falling to the ground, "Took me five years to master."

"Five years, you don't say."

"What are you doing?"

"Can't go to sleep thought I might need to walk around the island once or twice."

"Oh, okay, I'll walk with you."

After a long time of not talking, we came to the edge of the island, and subconsciously agreed to turn around.

"Be honest," Timmore suddenly said looking me in the eye. "That story was about you, wasn't it?"

"It was that obvious?" I said with a nervous chuckle, realizing why he was the former leader of the group.

"Oh, sure," Timmore replied, "You might have had the little ones fooled, but you didn't fool Berry, Cravon, and me."

I became even more nervous by the second. The kids knew that I was a sham, now what?

"I just want to say," he was about to say, but I interrupted him.

"I'm sorry," I confessed. "I'm not the hero you thought I was. I'm not worthy of your admiration, and I'm certainly not worthy of leading you guys."

I didn't want to cry in front of the kid. I tired holding the tear back for a second time.

"I just wanted to say," Timmore repeated, "That we honor how honest you were before us."

My ears perked up.

"You see," Timmore continued. "Before we were on this island, we believed our heroes could do no wrong. They were our idols. They were the reason we signed up to fight in 'the war', but one day, everything changed. We soon realized, despite all the villainy they enacted, our 'heroes' still masqueraded themselves as 'the good guys'."

Timmore took another deep breath before continuing.

"We soon saw the war for what it really was. Our 'heroes' said that the neighboring lands had refused to give their treasure to our supreme leader Kharull. We would sail on a ship, dock in a secret place, and attack the local towns to take off with their valuables. It seemed like only us kids felt like what we were doing was wrong."

My eyes widened. I wanted to tell him what Helina told me, but how could I? I agreed to myself it wouldn't be the right time to tell him just yet.

"It was horrible," he continued. "We had planned to escape, until the pirates attacked the ship."

"We began to think there was no difference between heroes or villains, but then we met you. We've never met someone before like you. You might have done some terrible things, but you saved us. Not only did you save us, but you were honest with us, even if you thought we would no longer want anything to do with you. I can't express what a relief it is to finally find someone who we can trust in. Thank you, Sir Wilhelm."

There was nothing I could say. I gave the boy a hug that my father once gave my eldest brother, and I patted him on the back. In response the boy patted mine. We walked slower than usual at that point. I looked up into the stars and wished that Helina was there to be with us.

"That girl who was with you, was she your best mate?" Timmore asked.

"Yep," I said choking up just thinking about her. "We were."

"Don't worry Sir," Timmore replied, "Now we can be best mates."

"Thanks kid," I said, and that was the last of our conversation. We both went back to our separate leaves and slept. For once in a long time, my mind was blissfully at ease, as the island's lulla-bye wisped me away into a relaxing slumber.

# Chapter iX

"Wake up, Sir Wilhelm, wake up," the kids screamed in my ear. I felt soft blows from their punches. I turned from one side to the other, pitifully failing to avoid their punches.

"Alright, alright, I'm awake, I'm awake," I pleaded. I opened my eyes to see the boys surrounding me.

"Ready to set sail Mr. Wilhelm?" asked Samuel I as I got up from my spot.

"Let me just have a small bite to eat, and I'll be ready for action," I answered.

After eating a fruit or two, I helped the kids pack all of our supplies on to the boat. I saw the golden genie lamp being placed into the pile. Something didn't feel right about bringing it along.

"Listen kids," I said getting their attention, "I know this goes without saying, but just to make sure we're clear, do not let the boar out under unless I say so."

The boys nodded their head understanding the grave effects of such an action.

Other than the lamp, our supplies consisted of fruits, and about twenty-eight purified water jugs (the boys were given two water jugs each before the escape). When everything was all accounted for, it was time for the boys to get their places and ready their oars.

"Lift the anchor!" I commanded.

"Lifting the anchor," said James doing so.

I got behind the boat and pushed, and, with the help of Samuel I and Mark, I was lifted into it. I carefully walked to the front in order to direct the ship. Every once in a while, I would look back to see the now desolate island. The smooshed trees became like twigs, and the sandy beach was about the size of a shield laying on its side. A couple of minutes later, the trees were no longer visible, leaving only a small dot on the horizon. I looked back for the very last time, only to see the island was finally out of site.

*What now?* I thought realizing the position I had gotten myself and the kids into. I couldn't believe how small minded I was. Being so caught up in getting off the island, I had forgotten to figure out where we would sail to. My first time actually being a leader, and I was sending myself and a bunch of kids to death.

*Snap out of it!* I thought to myself *We'll come to land sooner or later. But what if we don't? What then?*

"Are you okay Wilhelm?" asked Timmore concerningly.

"Yeah, I'm good," I said hiding my nervousness. "Say, you wouldn't know if there's any land nearby?"

"I don't know," he replied honestly; suddenly it smacked him right in the face. His mouth gaped, realizing the danger we were in. "What do we do?" he whispered to me.

"How about we pretend where we're going," I whispered back.

"You mean to lie?" he asked horrified.

"Listen," I told him, "How do you think the boys will react once we tell them we have no idea where we're going?"

"Uh, guys," I heard Berry say.

"We can always turn back," Timmore suggested ignoring Berry.

"Guys..." Berry said once again.

"Turn back?" I whispered in shock, "We can't turn back! Even if we do, we'll have no idea if we'll make it back to the island."

"GUYS!" Berry shouted.

"What?" Timmore and I asked. We saw a grave look on Berry's face

"We have company," he stated.

I turned my head, searching the horizon.

"Where?" I asked.

"Right there," Berry said pointing to a tiny silhouette of a ship, to the east.

"Is it a pirate ship?" Timmore asked aloud.

"Pirates?" Robert asked in fear.

"Not pirates," Samuel I squealed.

Well it was official. We were all scared out of our wits.

"Come on guys it might be a fishing ship," I remarked.

"How do you know?" Berry asked.

"Let's find out," I replied.

"But they'll see us," Mark stated in fear.

"As long as we keep our distance we'll be fine," I remarked. "If they are pirates we'll turn back around, okay? Look, we're in a tiny boat. They probably won't see us at all."

"You sure?" Berry asked.

"Have I ever steered you guys wrong?" I remarked, and that was the end of that. The closer we got to it, the more desperately I hoped that I was right, for a change.

We were only a few miles away from them, when we heard a crowd of men singing their hearts out, accompanied by a loud accordion.

> *"Whiskey from an old tin can,*
> *Whiskey Johnny!*
> *I'll drink whiskey when I can,*
> *Whiskey for my Johnny!"*

"Sounds like pirate singing," Berry commented.

"Fishermen sing all the time," I argued.

As the ship became bigger, we were able to make out the giant windows that would let sunlight into the captain's quarters. The railings were bright turquoise, the reflection of the ocean made the glass appear bright sky blue. We looked up to see their flag, but we weren't able to make heads or tails of it from the angle we were at.

"Looks like a pirate ship to me," Berry remarked.

"Let's don't jump to conclusions," I stated. "It's not like any of us have seen an actual pirate ship before. This might be a navy ship from some far-off land."

We floated closer. No one was steering the ship, and no one sitting in the rat's nest, but we could still here the choir of merry men singing.

*"A glass of grog for every man,*
*Whiskey, Johnny!*
*And a bottle for the chanteyman,*
*Whiskey for my Johnny!"*

Our boat was so close to the ship, we only needed a few more feet to touch the wood it was made of.

I was tempted to let the boat drift even closer, but then somebody popped his head over the edge. He was a rabbit, with his left ear chipped off, and the other one had a golden ring clasped onto it. He opened his mouth, and an orange chunky liquid flowed out.

"Aye, matey looks like his Johnny had too much whisky!" shouted someone on deck.

"Okay, let's turn around," I said realizing the danger that I had blinded myself to.

"Captain," the bunny exclaimed, "I see a tiny ship behind us."

"Now you've had too much." We assumed it was the captain replying, "Come back and sing with us."

"No, really it's right there," the bunny said. "Come look for yerself."

We all crossed our fingers hoping the captain didn't believe him.

"Well blow me down," we heard the presumed captain say, "Oye! Who are ye, and what be ye business?"

"Don't answer," I whispered to the boys. "They might leave us alone."

For a couple of minutes or two, it worked. It was easy and quiet sailing.

Then out of nowhere we heard a loud *BOOM!* We looked behind us and saw the pirate ship had turned to one side, and a black dot zoomed straight out of it. No wait, it wasn't a black dot; it was a cannon ball, and it headed right for us!

The cannon ball went directly over our heads, and splashed a couple of feet in front of us.

We heard the captain shout something, but he was too far away to hear him properly.

"What?" I shouted in reply. The captain yelled again, but we still couldn't hear him.

"Hold on," I replied, "Let us get closer so we can hear you."

I didn't need to tell the kids to row towards the ship; we had no choice.

We arrived about eight feet away from the ship. The entire crew were leaning on the railing to see the sight of us.

"What did you say?" I asked trying to find the captain in the bunch. I thought it would have been easy to pick him out of the crowd, but who knew all pirates looked the same.

"I said," said a scruffy looking creature with a brown beard, an eye-patch over his left eye, and a black cap over his head, "Who are ye, and what be ye... wait a minute. That voice, I've heard it before, but, no, it can't be. Rüpert!"

A Labrador with dirty fur walked towards the captain.

"Aye, sir?" he asked.

"Get me my spy-glass," the captain demanded.

"Aye, sir," the Labrador replied, heading towards the quarters. In less than a minute the dog was back out, holding a golden tube-like object in his paws.

"Your spy-glass, sir," he announced handing it off.

"Thank ye," the captain said receiving it. He placed it over his eye, and looked directly at me.

"By Davey Jones himself," the captain said with his mouth agape, "Youngest brother Wilhelm, tis that be ye?"

"What?" the kids and the pirate crew responded at once.

"I don't know this guy," I tried to tell them.

"Tis I, thou elder brother Wilhelm," he answered with excitement.

"But that can't be," I told him, "My elder brother was... kidnaped by... pirates. Wait how do I know you're just pulling my leg? Tell me something only my elder brother would know."

"Remember when ye accidently stained the royal tapestry when ye were little?" he asked not waiting for a response. "Tis I was that took the blame."

Suddenly, I saw the captain in a new light. He was a lemming like me, I imagined him without the beard and the eye patch, and there he was.

"Brother!" I exclaimed, "What are you doing here?"

"I should ask the same of ye," he replied, "Sitting in a rat trap of a boat with children, fruits, and silver jugs. Come up here along with thou little friends. We have a lot to talk about we do. Bring down the ladders!"

"Bringing down the ladders!" a weasel with a hook for a paw replied.

The kids still gave me weird looks as if they didn't know what to think.

"Are you sure about this Wilhelm?" Timmore asked concerned.

"Don't worry about it," I assured him, "He's a good guy. He's my brother after all. Nothing bad will happen."

# CHAPTER X

The crew gave us a big welcome with drunken cheer and laughter. Despite their warm greeting, me and the boys felt uncomfortable. The whole crew seemed like they had seen better days. The bunny, who we later learned was named Greifer the Chipped, only had five to seven teeth left. Rüpert Patch, had fur that was so rotten it was peeling off. There was also a cat named One Claw Svelt (Si-fet), not only did he have one claw for a paw, but his left leg was bent at a ninety-degree angle, forcing him to take a pause in-between steps.

The ship was a completely different creature altogether. Some of the floorboards were poking out, the deck didn't look like it had been cleaned in ages, there were gnats everywhere, and a terrible smell killed any sense of smell left.

"Welcome aboard *The Executioner*," my brother announced to us. He snatched a wooden jug from of one his pal's clutches, and raised it high in the air.

"To my long-lost brother," he announced, "And his wee little friends; may their time here be merry and peaceful,"

"Here, here," his crew replied before chugging down their drinks.

My brother finished by whacking his mug on the nearest barrel, and giving a loud burp, which sent the younger kids into fits of giggles.

"Oh, that's some good whiskey right there," he said contented, "Now, let's see if we can give ye little ones some room here. Shouldn't be too hard; just have to kill a few men first."

He and his crew laughed in unison.

"Don't mind me," he assured the kids. "That was just a joke, see. But for real now, Rüpert!"

"Aye, captain?" he asked.

"Find my brother's little friends some place to rest," my brother ordered, "If ye can't find room, make room."

"Aye, captain," Rüpert replied.

"Now go on kids, follow Rüpert," my brother said encouragingly.

"But what about Sir Wilhelm?" Timmore asked concerned.

"Don't worry about him," my brother assured. "He and I have some catching up to do. Run a long now."

"Don't worry Timmore," I told him. "Keep watch on the boys for me, okay?"

"Yes, sir," Timmore said before catching up with Rüpert.

"You'll be staying in my quarters for the time being," my brother said while turning around.

"Oh, I don't want to intrude," I told him.

"No, no I insist, that's what family is for, here have a drink."

He gave me his mug. I took it and gulped it down. I thought if my brother and his crew could handle it, so could I. Boy, was I wrong. It was the sourest drink I had ever tasted! I puked it all out to the ocean. My brother and the crew laughed at me.

"Ye land lover," my brother laughed wiping a tear from his eyes, "Couldn't hold it down, could ye? It was just a jest, anyway, how's the family doing?"

I then proceeded to tell him about everything that had happened to me in the past few weeks, or was it months? We walked past two weasels pulling our tiny ship out of the water and placing it near their spare escape wooden row boats. Throughout my whole story my brother didn't interrupt or utter a single word. For a moment, it seemed like I was leading him to the captain's quarters, not the other way around.

By the time I finished my story, we had arrived at our destination, and my brother opened the door for me. I walked in, and I was suddenly astonished with what I saw.

Unlike the outside of the ship that was decomposing by the seams, the room was all cleaned down to every corner. The railings on the wall were golden, and the floor was covered with red carpet free of stains or dirt. In the center of the room, there was a slick wooden desk, covered with various maps and other forms of documents. Standing by the window was a big round globe, with land masses I barely even recognized and the words were so small I would have needed a magnify glass to read them. Near the left side of the cabin rested a giant wooden bed. It had blue curtains hanging above it, and the bright red blankets were neatly placed on top, with two or three pillows to complete it.

I ran my paws through the bed curtains on impulse.

"It's a beauty ain't it?" my brother asked with a sense of pride.

"How did this happen?" I asked. "I told you my story, now you tell me yours."

My brother let out a long sigh.

"I guess there's no hiding it from ye now," he finally said. "Take a seat brother, t'is is going to be a long story."

I sat down on a curvy, wooden chair that was near the bed and was facing the direction of my brother. As he spoke, my brother would walk from one part of the room to the other, before taking a pause every now and again.

"As you know, when eldest brother died, I was declared future king of Rulksferd. Remember that day? The citizens cheered and celebrated. It seemed the only creature who wasn't happy, was me. Me being a king? How boring could ye get? Wake up, eat, sit down, listen to people complain and tell ye what ye should or shouldn't do, eat, sit down again, eat, and go to bed. What type of life is that? No life, that's what.

"Not only did I keep that secret from you and the family, but I was friends with a pirate captain, Captain Smocks. I loved the ocean, Wilhelm. I wanted to explore it all, instead of rotting in a castle all day. Me and

Smocks put our heads together and we planned my kidnaping. Just like you and Drovell planed your assassination. The rest you probably figured out for yourself."

"Dad was worried sick about you," I said digging my paws into the arm rests. "All that worrying was worthless?"

"Dad wouldn't have understood," my brother argued. "I didn't want to be king and neither did ye. At least when the citizens think of me, they remember me as a saint, but when the citizens think of ye, they'll remember ye as a devil. So, the way I see it, I got the sweet end of the deal."

"I can't believe what I'm hearing," I said not knowing whether to be horrified or angry. "You were not like this, never in my wildest dreams would I have imagined you saying what you just said."

"I have been like this," my brother revealed. "No one can act kind and be a proper gentle creature for every single day for the rest of their lives."

"Funny," I said getting up from my chair, "And to think, father's fur turned grey looking for you."

I don't know what I would have done if it weren't for the knock on the door.

"Come in," my brother answered.

The door opened to reveal One Claw Svelt shaking down to his paws.

"Captain," he said with a gulp, "You might want to see this."

My brother rushed outside, and I, not wanting the conversation to end, followed. All the crew members were frozen in their tracks. They all looked west where a small ship could be seen in the distance. The sails were dark and jagged. The ships had sharp bows that could pierce through rock.

"Great," my brother grunted, "Just great."

A loud trumpet like blast could be heard coming from the tiny ship in the distance, and the sounds of drums beating at a rhythmic beat followed. Turning to about a ninety-degree angle, there was no doubt that the ship was headed straight for us.

"Who are they?" I asked my brother putting our differences aside for the moment.

"They're followers of Kharull," my brother replied, "Don't know where they came from, but they just appeared one day, and they've been terrorizing the seas ever since. We destroyed one of their pillaging ships quite a while ago. It was a stormy night and they wanted to raid our ship. I should have expected word would get through. It seems like they've declared war on us."

I looked out to the ocean to see the sails coming closer. They were a dark red color and now that I saw them up close they reminded me of dragon wings from picture books.

"How long has it been since ye have swung a sword?" my brother asked.

"Not for a long time," I said looking back at him.

"Well, practice makes perfect, as they say," he said giving a grin. My brother turned to the crew to give them his plan of action. I tried to pay attention, but something was drawing me towards the enemy ship. I heard voices calling out to me.

*"Sir Wilhelm!"* they said, *"Sir Wilhelm!"*

I shook my head. Maybe the whiskey I had before was finally getting to me, but I just needed to find out what was drawing me towards the ship.

"Excuse me, brother," I said right in the middle of his master plan.

"What?" he asked frustrated, "Can't you see I'm planning here?"

"May I have your spy-glass?" I asked him.

"Oh, yeah sure," he replied, "Rüpert, give me brother me spy-glass."

"Aye sir," Rüpert replied before walking off. A moment later he came back and handed it to me. I thanked him before putting it over my eye and looking towards the enemy ship.

There it was in all its glory, the golden chandelier! Instead of four glowing diamonds there were five. I suddenly noticed a familiar face. No wait! It was Helina's face, and it was coming from the red diamond that was placed next to the last empty holder! I needed to see more.

Bringing the spy-piece upward, who was there but the pointy mustache ferret himself, Dhikrullah. He was shouting towards at his men, and of half them drawn out their swords. The archers picked up bags of arrows and headed straight towards a lit torch that was hanging on a pole below the main sail.

I put down spy-glass and tapped my paw on my brother's shoulder.

"What is it now littlest brother?" he asked frustratingly, "I already gave ye the spy-glass."

"You need to take a look at this," I said, handing the eye glass to him. He grungily took it from me and looked towards Dhirkullah's ship.

"Oh, my," he said after swearing under his breath. "If they fire those things, our entire ship will be toast!"

"Fire at them, before they fire at us!" a skinny mouse named Frelon announced. Some of the crew cheered in agreement.

"We can't," my brother said putting the spy-piece down to his side, "They're too close to us now. If we hit them it will take us a minute to reload the canons. It will only take them a few seconds to reload their bows. Even with our muskets, I doubt we'll be able to take down every signal archer before our ship burns in flames. We have no choice but to surrender. I'm sorry there's no other way."

We waited for the enemy ship to come closer to us. The beating of the drums became louder and louder, until stopping abruptly when the enemy ship appeared only a foot away from us.

"Ahoy there," my brother greeted, "What ye business be?"

Dhikrullah walked down to the main deck of his ship.

"Our business," he announced, "Is with you. You attacked one of our vessels a few nights ago. Not only did you attack them, but you killed them as well."

"Nothing personal," my brother interrupted, "A pirate's life is kill or be killed."

"Same with us," Dhikrullah replied, "But you are a gang of fools. Not only were you to foolish enough to attack one of our own, but you have the gall to have a magic golden lamp in your possession."

My brother looked confused. My stomach sank into the ocean. It was my fault; I shouldn't have brought the lamp with us in the first place.

"What lamp?" my brother asked the ferret. "We might have taken many priceless treasures, but a magical lamp aint' one of them."

"Do not lie, especially to me," Dhikrullah said scowling. "I know you have our lamp. We've been tracking it for weeks. We had it in our clutches one time, until a little intruder took if from us. We've followed the path to the seas, and now it has brought us to you."

"I don't know how ye be able to sniff out a made up 'magical lamp'," my brother exclaimed, "But on my pirate's honor, I swear, it is not here."

"Then your honor is useless," Dhikrullah said. "If you won't comply, then I'll have no choice but to slice the necks of every single one of ya, take the lamp, and burn this ship to the very last splinter. Understand?"

"Aye," my brother agreed, "Come on aboard,"

"That's more like it," Dhikrullah said satisfied. While we prepared to be boarded, a tiny idea popped into my head.

"Brother," I whispered, "We'll lead them to the bottom deck and then we'll kill them all."

"No," he said frustrated, "It's too risky, plus they'll be expecting it. Let them scour the boat, and once they realize that what they're looking for is not here, they'll leave like nothing happened."

Without a clear plan to go on, I scurried below the deck. If my brother wasn't going to listen to me, then the kids would. I found them wandering in the next to bottom level, where all the cannons were kept.

"We're in trouble," I told them.

"What is it Sir Wilhelm?" Timmore asked, the other kids looked concerned.

"The followers of Kharull are boarding this very ship," I said before I heard gasps from the kids.

"We can't go back to them, we just can't," Simon II pleaded.

"Don't worry," I assured them all, "It will take a while before they come down here. Enough to time to come up with a plan! Let's put our heads together to see what we can come up with."

The enemy ship was resting next to us. We were in a room with seven canons. I walked back to the ladder leading to the second level. I didn't notice it before, but each section below the deck had a wooden hatch. They could only be locked from the inside; my brother must have had the master key. If we could trap Dhikrullah and company in the level between where the canons were and the upper deck, place objects on top of the hatch, and lock the main entrance to the upper deck from the outside, then, we had the upper paw.

"Kids come here," I told them, "I think we have a plan that might just work."

They all ran to me and listened intently to what I had in store. Once I finished they were all impressed and started chipping in with ideas of their own. I only wished we had more time to get everything down to the last detail, but we all knew Dhikrullah and his men would be coming any second.

The kids quietly, but quickly, scurried to their positions, all except Timmore who stood right by my side.

"Now remember," I told him, "do not unlock the hatch until you hear my knock, understand?"

"Yes, Sir Wilhelm," he replied.

I was about to ask them if they had ever worked a canon before, but I heard paw-steps right above our heads. I took a deep breath. It was either now or never. I grabbed hold of the ladder and went up to the second level. Once I had my paws on the floor, I heard the *thunk* of the hatch locking into place.

In front of me was a corridor of hammocks, and no doubt that Dhikrullah's group were just around the corner.

"Hey, Dhikrullah!" I shouted to the other end of the room. Their steel swords were drawn out of their scabbards.

"Well, well," I heard Dhikrullah say. He took long and slow steps, as he walked around the corner. He was so far away that it almost looked like he walked out of the wall.

"You are a sight for sore eyes," he continued, "Honestly, did you think you could escape from me?"

"How did you find me?" I asked him. He began to chuckle in response.

"Simple, really," he finally said, "The scent of genie magic is subtle, but can be recognized if one is familiar with it. Uknamra is an expert on tracing such a scent, so when you disappeared, it was just a matter of time before my second in command found you out. Now hand it over."

"Over my dead body," I said bolting towards them. They almost caught me. I zoomed passed the corner, and floated up the ladder, outside onto the deck.

I slammed the two doors, I commanded the first two guys to keep the doors closed.

"Brother," my brother said in shock, "What are ye doing?"

"Saving our hide," I replied. I headed straight for Dhikrullah's ship.

"Listen up," I shouted at the scoundrels, "Your leader and his posy are locked within our ship with nowhere to go. I have seven cannons pointed at you guys right now, each stationed by critters ready to light the match and sink your tiny sail boat to the ocean floor. If you attack us, not only do you bring death to your leader, but death to yourselves. If you drop your weapons, and surrender, we will spare your lives. Now which is it?"

The arches and the crew looked at each other. I heard a sword jam through the two doors, but the two brutes pushed back. The archers put down their bows and arrows, and raised their paws in the air.

I couldn't believe it. I had no idea I had such great strength in me. The crew was dumbfounded, while my brother gave me an angry stare.

*What's your problem?* I thought, *I just saved us all, and captured the villain and his goons. What's so bad about that?*

# CHAPTER XI

As the stars glimmered in the night sky, I was standing in the very bottom level, below the canons. Next to the storage shed was a little jail cell resting in the corner, keeping Dhikrullah and his crew smooshed inside. The space was so small they could barely stretch their legs.

I looked at Dhikrullah eye to eye. I felt the flames of his anger scorching my fur.

"You know," he said to me, "If I had known how much of an annoyance you would become, I would have killed you the moment I saw you."

"Your loss my gain," I replied. All the questions I wanted to ask him danced in my head. There were so many, I had no idea where to start.

"What is that golden object?" I asked him. "The one holding the diamonds."

"I don't have to tell you anything. "He answered before spitting at my face.

"You know I'm not stupid," I told him. "You use the diamonds to contain the captured genies and that golden object syphons their power, which ends in you ruling the world. Is that right?"

"It won't matter," he replied, "You're just putting off the inevitable. The more I'm behind these bars, the more you will suffer. The legacy of Kharull will rise, and not even a filthy wretch like you can stop me!"

"Don't you see where you are?" I asked rhetorically. "You're locked up; we caught you. You lost; we won. It's over."

"Oh, but it's far from over," he said licking his lip, "It won't be long now till you set us free. You may laugh, but I swear to you it will happen, very soon now. You'll be sorry that you ever messed with me, very sorry indeed."

Something told me that I wouldn't be getting any answers from him. As I climbed up the ladder to the deck I could still hear his voice in my head.

*"It won't be long now . . . very soon now . . . you'll be sorry . . . very sorry indeed."*

\*\*\*

The crew was having the time of their lives. Amongst all the merriment, I strangely felt out of place.

*Come on, Wilhelm, get it together* I told myself *You won, enjoy yourself.*

But try as I might, I could never get myself to be a part of the festivities. Two from my brother's crew carried the golden chandelier like object onto the deck. Bringing the thing onto *The Executioner* made sense, but if Dhikrullah knew he was going to be set free then maybe it wasn't okay bringing the object closer to him.

"Youngest brother Wilhelm!" my brother exclaimed knocking me out of my thoughts, "Come with me I have something I want to tell ye, brother to brother."

"Sure, why not?" I said forcing a smile onto my face. He pushed me past the crew, and into his quarters. After closing the door behind me, he stepped in front of me and looked at me face to face. His hands jumped out, and held on to my collar with a strong grip.

"Who do you think you are?" he asked with a growl.

"Your brother," I answered with a small chirp.

"Don't be funny with me," he said slamming me against the door, "Ye think ye can come on to my ship, and start acting like ye own the place?"

"I don't understand," I said completely confused.

"How dare ye give me that," my brother said offended. "Ye ordered those Dhikrullah's around men like ye were the captain of *my* ship! I've been living my dream, and I won't let ye take it away from me!"

"But I don't want your dream," I said earnestly. "Being a pirate is the last thing on my list."

"Ye made me look like a fool in front of me own crew," my brother explained. "Now they'll always look back on this moment and think 'Remember when we captured Dhikrullah and his men? Oh yeah, Captain Wilhelm's younger brother was sure brave and smart. Where was the captain? Why wasn't he just as brave and just as smart like his younger brother?' See what you've done? Ye ruined my reputation! Ten years of building my persona out the window! Do you understand?"

My head hung low. I didn't know what to say, or how to feel. A feeling of shame overwhelmed me, without really knowing what I should have been ashamed about. Was it worrying if my older brother was perfectly safe, or overstepping my bounds by being a leader over a ship that wasn't mine?

"I understand," I said with a sigh. "I'm sorry."

"Good," my brother said nodding his head, "Now if ye don't mind, I'll be calling the shots here. After all, I am the captain."

With that, he adjusted his coat and walked outside. The door would have slammed in my face if I hadn't caught it in time. My brother really didn't expect me to stay in his quarters, did he? He didn't give any orders, so I had every right to follow him.

The whole crew was scrambling around, almost as if in a blind panic.

"What's going on?" I shouted over the noise.

"Hurry now, I want to see ye near those canons right now!" I heard my brother screaming out. This was the only answer I needed to figure out what was going on.

"Wait, you're going to blow up the ship?" I asked him in shock.

"Are ye by the canons men?" he shouted ignoring my question.

"You can't do that," I pleaded with him. "I promised if they surrendered, we wouldn't destroy their ship!"

"Ye might have promised them," my brother said to me, "But I didn't. Ready the canons!"

"Canons ready," someone shouted from below deck.

"Fire at will!" he shouted.

Within seconds Dhikrullah's ship exploded into millions of pieces. My brother grinned, as if to say, "What are you going to do now?"

I felt a burning anger at him, I wanted to punch him in the face, but I held back as much as I could.

"Why did you do that?" I growled at him.

"I'm the captain of this ship!" my brother yelled into my ears. "I don't have to explain anything to ye."

I couldn't stand the sight of him. I stormed off in a blaze. I needed to calm down. I needed to talk to someone who I could talk to, someone who would understand.

***

"Can you believe it?" I asked Helina after ranting for what seemed like an hour. I took her diamond out of the chandelier to the corner of the third level below the ship, with only a stack of crates separating us from the cell.

Helina's body was the size of my finger. If she wasn't trapped in the red diamond someone could have squashed her like a bug. Her back leaned against the glass.

"Well it makes sense," she finally said.

"What?" I said surprised "You mean you're on his side?"

"I'm not on anybody's side," she clarified "Think about it from his perspective. Once the rest of Dhikrullah's men know that he's missing, they'll know he was captured at sea, they'll send all their ships out here and once they find us we'll be the ones taken prisoner. The only way to stop that is to keep moving and destroying the evidence."

"Why didn't my brother tell me that in the first place?" I asked her.

"Why didn't you tell him about your scheme to capture Dhikrullah or that you had smuggled my lamp?" she pointed out.

"Because he would have stopped me," I told her. "He was talking about surrendering. For all he knew, Dhikrullah could have killed us all. I wasn't going to stand by and give them that chance."

"He was the captain, Wilhelm, and still is," Helina replied. "Put yourself in his shoes. No one is as black and white as we would want them to be. See the situation from both sides, like a self-less creature would do."

Only her words could be allowed to settle into my mind like they did.

"To think," Helina continued, "Dhikrullah could have been a son of an innocent merchant, a farmer, or someone who knew a decent trade. He had a future and a loving family; but thanks to my blindness, I took all of that away from him. Now he's an angry ferret, who no longer has a family and is bent on restoring the rule of an animal not worthy of such idolization, all because of me."

She began to weep softly against the walls of her diamond prison cell. I never took that into consideration before. When Helina first mentioned it, when we were on the island, I had hardly thought of it as something of importance.

"It's not your fault," I told her. "That was Kharull's fault; he used you."

"If I didn't let him use me, none of us would be in this mess," she exclaimed.

"True," we heard a voice say in reply. Helina and I turned our heads to see Timmore looking at us with his wide eyes, "I could have been with my father, my mother, or with any of my brothers if I had any. But then, I wouldn't get to meet Sir Wilhelm, and I wouldn't be here thanking you for saving us from the Great Mighty Boar."

"It was mostly Wilhelm who did the saving," Helina pointed out, wiping the last tear from her eye.

"Right again," Timmore said in reply, "But he wouldn't have been on that island if you hadn't moved him there. The who would have gotten the magic lamp to suck the monster into it?"

"What's your name?" Helina asked

"Timmore, Miss," he answered.

"I should be thanking you, Timmore," Helina said earnestly, "And you, Wilhelm, for giving me assurance that I'm not some stupid, naive, lynx."

Even though I was not able to hug her, hugging the diamond would have had to do for the moment, and for just that moment, all time had stopped. Whatever the future had in store for us, could wait. We treasured this moment as long it had lasted.

\*\*\*

The rising sun singled the new day for *The Executioner*. For me it was the first time I had slept in with a comfortable bed in weeks. I forgot how soft the blankets were, or how fabric felt so smoothly on a pillow.

At first glance, it almost felt like I was inside my castle, but when the floor rocked up and down, I remembered that I was still on my brother's ship. I had no idea when I went to bed, or how I got into the cabin. To be honest I didn't remember anything else after putting Helina's diamond back on to the golden chandelier. I must have let myself in sometime after that, but only my brother could say for certain.

I forced the covers off my body and placed both paws on the floor. More aware of my surroundings, I noticed two chairs, both facing each other, with a blanket resting on one of them. A blanket lied still in front of the chairs. Maybe I had given my brother too little credit. What else was he sacrificing because of my intrusion on his life?

Opening the door, I was greeted by the bright blue sky above me. Two pirates, a koala named Blue Tooth and a goat named Martin Hammer, were playing a game of chess, or something that looked like it. The board was torn up, the colors faded, and the pieces were weathered beyond recognition.

"Where's the captain?" I asked Martin.

His eyes were twitched like crazy. I had no idea if he was looking at the board or at me.

"You'll find him at the wheel," he replied.

It wasn't long until I was walking up the steps and standing next to my brother who had his paws around the helm.

"Good morning brother," he said greeting me.

"Hey," I replied. "Listen, about last night, you were right about everything. I had no right to take over like that. I should have told you about the lamp."

"I'm the one who's sorry," my brother said taking me off guard. "I had too much to drink that night. I shouldn't have lashed out at you like that."

I wanted to say something more, but I couldn't find the words to say. For the next few minutes we just looked at the vast oceanic horizon rhythmically sway up and down. We saw Samuel II and James running around the deck playing a game of tag.

"Look at those young'ins over there," my brother finally said. "Remember when we were that age Wilhelm? Those were the days. No responsibilities, pure unadulterated freedom without a care in the world, nothing like being king."

"Yeah," I agreed, "But someone has to do it. I've tried forgetting about Rulksferd, but I left it in such a heaping mess. I want to go back and - I don't know -

maybe restore it to the way it was before I screwed everything up."

"That's why ye should have left before father died," my brother suggested. "Ye should have tagged along with your other brother to the monastery."

I imagined my father lying in bed, all alone with only his servants by his side, not a single loved one being there for his last day on earth. It gave me cold chills thinking about dying such a death.

"A pirate ship is not fit for children," my brother suddenly stated. "They would fit nicely at Blue Wall Abbey; let all the monks take care of them."

"I wonder if our other brother is there," I pointed out. "He never stated which monastery he went to, just that he became a monk."

"That may be," my brother replied. "I'm also thinking of dropping off that *object* to the Abbey as well. They've been known to protect magical objects throughout the world."

"But first let's leave Dhikrullah and his men on that deserted island you came from."

"Alright," I replied. Personally, I didn't like the idea, but my brother was the captain.

Our conversation continued for a pretty long time until we finally heard the "land hoe" from the rat's nest. My brother ordered Dhikrullah and his men out of the cell.

"Dhikrullah," he said once the deed was done, "Consider yerself lucky I'm not making ye walk the plank."

"You will wish you had," he shouted. "Once my fleet find me, I'll kill you myself!"

"Yeah, yeah, whatever," my brother said under his breath, "Get this garbage off my ship."

His crew forced Dhikrullah and his men off of the ship and onto the once luscious island. When the very last of them was off, and we took headed for Blue Wall Abbey, glad that we would never see Dhikrullah or his little army again.

# CHAPTER XII

The bright sunset gave the waves a golden tint. My last moments on *The Executioner*, were spent with glee and happiness. I played with the kids, sang and danced with the crew, and helped out with life on the sea from cleaning the deck to preparing food. I had never pictured myself on a pirate ship, with my long-lost brother, but then again nothing in my life seemed to be going the way I expected.

Each of the boys got to meet Helina and thanked her for helping to defeat the mighty boar. We asked the other genies about their lives and how they were trapped in their emeralds.

Esmeralda, daughter of Orion, was a prairie dog who once lived in the desert village of Kryoden near the Peyote Kingdom. Her story was similar to Helina's in that the town fool, another prairie dog named Thomas son of Cointh, rubbed an empty genie lamp onto her fur, and she had no choice but to grant his every wish. Tom hated being classified as the town fool, so his first wish was to be smarter compared to everyone else in Kryoden. Once the wish was granted, Tom realized the differences between being smart and wise. So, his second wish was to be the wisest among all the citizens of the village. As soon as his wish was granted and realized that he had gained his wisdom through no means of his own, he wished to start as a fool again so he could work his way up to his wisdom. Thomas then gave Esmerlda's lamp to a vender, where she was sold as a lighting lamp until Dhikrullah found her.

Latasha, daughter of Marcus, was a wolf who lived in the cold north valley of Coreth. While traveling with her pack, she found an empty genie lamp in the snow. Not knowing what it was she rubbed some snow off it, causing the lamp to suck her inside. She, along with her lamp, were buried in the snow for what she claimed to be centuries. Latasha told us if she wasn't a spirit, she would have been frozen to death, especially since her multilayered coat was transformed into an outfit that left little to the imagination. When she was awakened by the sound of someone digging, she thought she was finally going to be rescued. These thoughts were shattered once she realized the creatures who rescued her, traded her golden prison for a diamond one.

Maxine, daughter of Gavol, occupied the green diamond. Her tale was not a glamorous one. She had lived in the desert city of Gamonesh and married a hamster named Ferlon, son of Trevon, just for his money. They had a terrible fight, and she used the abandoned genie lamp – which was just being used as a normal lamp – to strike him dead. To get rid of the evidence, she rubbed the blood off of the lamp. She believed being a genie was a form of punishment for her actions.

The occupant of the white diamond was a squirrel named Nymphira (Nim-fi-ra), daughter of Jenopha. She didn't say much, and she was the quietest of the bunch. She simply stated that her history as a genie was quite an eventful one, spanning over a thousand years. Nymphira's only memory before being a genie, was when she was a child stealing a lamp in a carriage from a traveling sales beaver.

As we continued to travel the deep blue sea, I began to wonder how we would get all the genies out of their diamond prisons. What would happen if they were set free? A frightening thought made my stomach churn. So much so, that I pushed it into the back of my mind as far as I could. But the thought would speak in a low whisper, letting me know my time with Helina would be coming to a close.

***

"Land hoe!" the pirate announced from the rat's nest.

The boys and I walked onto the deck, blinking once or twice in order to adjust to the evening sun. My brother ordered half the men to prepare to dock, while he order the other half to bring the golden chandelier up to the deck. It still bothered me even after all this time that I still didn't have a name for it. Not even Nyphira knew what it was called.

"There it is," my brother announced happily, "Blue Wall Abbey."

I turned around to see what my brother was talking about. To my disappointment, the walls were not blue, but a bright yellow with red tiles. There were watch towers placed on every corner. If I didn't know better it looked more like a valiant fortress run by warriors than a peaceful abbey run by monks.

"Why is it called Blue Wall Abbey again?" I asked my brother.

"Because it's near the sea, duh!" he said in a joking matter.

We entered into the abbey's port. Several creatures were wrapping up from their daily fishing trips. I followed the wooden pier to a giant door that sealed the monster sized gateway.

"Open the gates!" shouted a watchman.

"Opening the gates," another watchman shouted back.

With a loud thud, audible from miles away, the giant door slowly began to open.

Even when I squinted my eyes, I could barely make out the creatures walking towards us. A little pudgy one said something I couldn't understand; then he started running towards *The Executioner* in a mad dash. It was sort of funny watching him run, but as we both headed towards each other, my smile had faded into pure shock.

"No way," I said, "No way, no way, no way."

"What is it Sir Wilhelm?" Timmore asked curiously, while my brother gave a bellowing laugh.

I should have known that the ball of fur huffing and puffing his way toward us was my other brother, Wilhelm III.

"Brothers!" he said.

"Brother Wilhelm III?" I exclaimed still amazed.

"It is so wonderful to see you again," my brother said with joy. "I haven't seen both of you in ages. This calls for a celebration!"

"There's no need," I tried to explain, but my other brother wouldn't hear of it.

"We have an item of interest for you brother," my older brother exclaimed.

"I'll have a look at it soon enough," was the reply, "But once you and your men find good spot to anchor, we'll start the festivities immediately!"

My brother and I sighed. It was so nice to see him so happy and full of life. It reminded us both of when we were just meddlesome kids in the court room.

# CHAPTER XIII

A cheery flute sung in harmony with the strums of a lute and violin, as the tabor drummed in accompany with them. Conversations between friends and strangers filled the atmosphere. I had never seen such a feast since my days in the palace. The table was filled with roasted chickens, smoked turkeys, soaked salads, baked pastries, and sweetened delights for everyone, and then some. I was sitting next to my other brother, who I learned went up the ranks to become Father Wilhelm the Abbot. My and I were the guests of honor and were accommodated with the best seats in the house.

I looked at the wall every now and again, only to see fully armored guards holding spears in their paws eyeing the crowd.

"What's with the tight security?" I asked my brother.

"Well, usually when we have a feast something terrible happens," he explained. "After one celebration, the adults were knocked out with a sleeping gas, and all the orphans were kidnapped by villains. Another time, when everything seemed to be going well, until another group of baddies breached our walls and just about killed us all. Oh, there was this one time where..."

"Stop," I said with understanding, "I get it. Jeeze, how many enemies does this peaceful abbey have anyway?"

"When you're the sole protector of magic items, nefarious master minds seem to spring out of the ground," my brother explained, "But that's enough of the abbey's history, I want to know more about how the kingdom of Rulksferd is doing under your leadership."

"Yeah, funny story actually," I said in shame. I told my brother everything, while taking breaks to catch my breath, eat some food, or to take a breather.

"Well" he said, once I finished, "Rudding probably knows what he is doing. I'm sure Rulksferd is in good paws."

"But what if Rudding was counting on us to forfit the crown so he could rule Rulksferd himself?" I asked him.

"Listen, brother," he said, placing his cup down, "Being around magic long enough has proven to me that everything happens for a reason. Maybe a creature like

Rudding coming into power was bound to happen sooner or later. Maybe he's the ruler that Rulksferd needs right now."

"How do we know for sure? What if he isn't the right ruler for Rulksferd?"

"Brother, if you were an abbot like me, you would learn that it is easier to accept things the way they are and move on," he tried to explain to me.

"Then why did you forfeit the crown?" I argued. He looked like he was about to say something when the music died down, allowing the bugles to make their roaring announcement.

"Make way for Rathaetouy (Rath-a-tou-e) the Great!" the squire exclaimed. The abbots, the monks, the servants, and the abbey children started murmuring to themselves.

"Who's Rathaetouy?" Timmore asked.

"Only the awesome-st warrior of our generation!" exclaimed a monk.

"He's so awesome!" exclaimed a high-pitched voice. The female servants started to groom their fur, and my other brother sat up straighter.

The sound of armor clanking together grew louder and louder, as the entire group went quiet down.

The largest knight I had ever seen walked forward, followed by what looked like his squire. I assumed the squire was the red-tail squirrel, he wore green garments, similar to what all the other abbey children wore.

"Rathaetouy, oh how it is a joy to see you again," my brother announced.

"Thank you, Father Wilhelm," the red-tail squirrel chipped.

*Wait* I thought *That's Rathaetouy?*

"Rathaetouy, allow me to introduce you to my brother, Wilhelm VI," my brother exclaimed.

The red-tailed squirrel walked towards me.

"A pleasure to meet you sir," he said shaking my paw.

"The pleasure is all mine," I said just being polite.

"I've found where the Brosvenki Gang are Father Wilhelm," Rathaetouy said, now looking at my brother again. "By this time tomorrow, Fergully will see what's coming to him!"

The Abbey practically jumped in the air with a joyous cheer.

I gave my other brother a look that said, *"Brosvenki Gang? Fergully?"*

To which he replied with a look that said, *"I'll explain later."*

Rathaetouy pulled up a chair, and the singers started performing songs about his great heroics. Some included slaughtering dragons, bringing peace to the land, and slaying some of the vilest creatures of all kinds. For an animal so great, I had never heard of him before. I looked at my brother, the captain, and he looked bored beyond belief.

"A toast to Rathaetouy," Father Wilhelm said raising his cup, "The Abbey wouldn't be safer without you."

"Here, here," said the other animals. To be polite again, I raised my cup with the crowd, and gulped down the wine.

"Hey, Rathaetouy," I shouted towards him, "Have you ever traveled to Rulksferd?"

"Never heard of it before," he answered.

"You know the Starway River?"

"I don't know what you're talking about. Is that near Porter's Lake?"

"I'll show you a map some time."

"A map?" one of the abbots scoffed. "Rathaetouy doesn't need a map, he follows the stars and the moss on trees to find his way."

"Are you familiar with the constellation of Jinx?" I asked him. "The constellation only appears in spring, above the land of Rulksferd. It is said to depict Jinx the warrior flinging her arrows in battle."

"Of course, I know the consolation of Jinx," Rathaetouy said with a half-smile, "I know all of them."

"Forgive my brother," Father Wilhelm said suddenly. "In no way does he mean to insult your vast intelligence."

*Insulting his vast intelligence?* I thought raising my eye-brow. I was just asking a simple question.

"That's okay," Rathaetouy said shrugging it off. "I have heard that my greatness is hard to be comprehend for some creatures."

"Okay what's this all about?" I asked clearly insulted by his remark.

"Brother, could you come with me for a moment?" my other brother said getting out of his chair. Grudgingly I followed, while the kids looked turned their heads to see where I was going.

We were some distance from the festivities, when my brother told me everything.

"Listen," he explained, "I told you since Blue Wall Abbey protects all magical objects, we're constantly bombarded by enemies. In order to defend ourselves, the Abbey picks one of the orphans who shows the most promise, creates a prophecy around him, and raise him as the chosen one."

"Huh?" I said in disbelief, "So there's nothing great about this kid Rathaetouy?"

"Oh, no," he replied. "The kid has spunk. He has the warrior spirit. Plus, his family unfortunately died in a fire that consumed his whole village. He was the most depressed youngling this abbey had ever seen. Since we had not had a chosen one in a long time, and we needed a way to make him happy, we decided to make him a chosen one."

"Isn't that lying?".

"It is, but Wilhelm please, he hasn't been this happy for a long time, and we intend to keep him that way. This is how it's always been, and there's no need to go against it. So, no more questions about his knowledge, his skill, or his stories, okay?"

I wanted to say no way, but I couldn't just tell him no.

"Sure, I promise," I said, wondering thinking how long I could keep this new charade before telling Rathaetouy the truth.

\*\*\*

The party had faded, the flames died down, and the servants finished cleaning the aftermath of the festivities. My brother, the Abbot provided me with my own room, and the kids stayed with the other orphan children.

While heading to my room, I had to go through the tapestry hall, which held all the stories of the heroes of Blue Wall Abbey. My brother gave me a long list of heroes such as; Greyjoy the Strong, Clementine the Kind, Livendell the Wise, Melvin the Warrior, and, soon to be, Rathaetouy the Brave. Each illustration sewn on to the fabric was fascinating. I would have wanted to know the stories of all them a, but I never found the time.

My room was only large enough to have the bare essentials; a bed, a desk, and a window that faced the open sea. The only source of light in my dark room was a lit lantern on my desk. I was about to put it out when I heard a commotion outside my window. I poked my snout out to see *The Executioner* livelier than ever. Was my older brother leaving already? And without a goodbye, no less? I didn't know why, but I felt like I needed to be there to see him off.

I grabbed the lantern and headed out the door. Who knew an Abby could be so spooky at night. It was as if I was the only creature living in the entire building. I was even scared stiff by the site of my shadow once. Fortunately, the big gate leading to the dock, was still open. The dock was brightened by the light of several torches. I placed my lantern on the ground and started heading towards my brother's ship.

"Brother!" I yelled.

"Yes?" one brother asked turning his head towards me.

"No, the other one," I explained.

"Oye, brother," I heard him say from aboard the ship. It took me a second, but I finally saw staring down at me from the deck. "Want to sail the seas with me?"

"No," I answered, "I feel like I'm needed here."

"To each his own then," he said in reply. "You're call is here, the ocean is mine."

"Will I see you again?" I asked him.

"We might," he answered. "Who knows, we crossed paths once, who says we won't again?"

It was like when Helina was sucked into the skies during our fight with Great Mighty Boar. I had no idea if my brother would die shortly afterwards or live a long happy life.

"Don't worry about me brother," he said as if he had read my mind, "I know how fend for me-self. Lift the anchor!"

"Goodbye brother," I exclaimed, I felt my remaining brother placing his paw on my back. "Thank you, for everything."

"Tis was my pleasure," my brother replied, "So long, brothers."

We both waved to him, as *The Executioner* slowly moved out of the port.

"Don't worry," my other brother said reassuringly, "He'll come back. There may be more magical objects yet to be discovered."

I took in a deep breath, walked back and picked up my lantern, and then returned to my room.

As I slept on my small, yet comfortable bed, I fell asleep to the singing of the crew and the sounds of the ocean.

> *Whisky from the sun's golden rays,*
> *Whiskey, Johnny,*
> *I'll drink whiskey till my dying day*
> *Whiskey for my Johnny.*

# CHAPTER XIV

The ocean waters were rising, flooding my small room. I was swept away by the current and being driven out to sea. I tried moving my body, but it was of no use. The waters became violent, and monstrous waves splashed on to me.

I woke up with a start, immediately noticing my clothes and my bed were soaked to the core. The next thing I noticed was the ray of sunlight coming through the window. I rubbed my eyes, to see all the boys in my room, with Gerbert and Cravon holding an empty bucket. Each of the kids had mischievous smiles on their faces, while my brother gave a small chuckle.

"Why you little monsters," I cried with a grin, "Come here."

I then started chasing the kids around my room.

"I suppose you were behind this, weren't you?" I asked my brother giving him a small, harmless punch.

"I needed to get you up somehow," he said laughing his robes off, "If I had let you be, you would have probably slept for days."

"What time is it anyway?" I asked him.

"Almost midday," he answered.

"Almost midday?" I said surprised, "Good night!"

"You mean Good Day," my brother corrected. "If it makes you feel better, you have given our team of researchers more time to look into that magical object you and our other brother left behind."

After receiving a robe, I walked with my brother through the open hallways. I asked him why the entrances to each hallway had their own letter had chiseled on the top of the edge. He looked up, and he paused for a moment.

"Hmmm..." he said pondering the question, "I've never noticed that before, I'll ask around."

We trotted up a few steps, turned a few corners, and went down five or six corridors until we finally came to a wooden door. My brother gave several taps, before the animal on the other end opened the door.

He was an abbot, wearing the same brown robes my brother was wearing. He was a mouse with bright brown fur, and his snowy white whiskers were so untrimmed, they brushed against the door.

"Father Wilhelm come in, come in," he said urgently.

"Brother Montague, this is my brother Wilhelm IV," he said introducing me for, what the third, or fourth time.

"How you do, how you do?" the mouse said shaking my paws. With his weak grip, I was deathly afraid his paws would break off. I could make out all the veins throughout his withered arms.

Surprisingly, he had the strength to push the door even farther, allowing me and my brother through. The room was filled with podiums, holding up all sorts of magical objects; a levitating rug, a collection of potions, a bag that I was told, was bottomless, silver slippers that could transport the wearer anywhere if they clicked the heels together.

"Why's that podium barren?" I asked my brother.

"Oh, brother," he said laughing, "That's where the invisible cloak is kept."

Some more podiums held; a golden ring that was said to give ultimate power, a wizard's staff, a wooden chalice that was said to give eternal life to whoever drank from it, a small medallion that could take over the mind of anyone, a pot of flowers that could render someone to sleep with just one whiff, and finally the golden chandelier like object.

Next to the podium was another abbot in the same brown robes and towering over everyone in the room.

"Brother Stonegrave," my brother said announcing our presence.

"Greetings, Father Wilhelm," he said turning his entire body so he could face us, "And this must be your brother, Wilhelm IV."

"Yep, that's me," I said chipperly. Stonegrave reached for my paw, exposing his giant muscles. My face turned pale. Unlike Brother Montague, I was concerned my paws would be crushed into countless pieces!

I closed my eyes, waiting to lose all use of my paws, but thankfully he was easy on me, and loosened his grip, probably by a thousand.

I introduced him to the genies in the diamonds. Each of them replied with a "hello" or "how do you do?"

"So, what have you discovered so far about this queer object?" my brother asked him.

"Quite a lot Father, given the amount of time we've spent already," he answered. "From what my team has gathered, this object is called the Ynjusay (Yin-joo-say), it's a Gamoneshian term which means; The Genie Syphoner. It was made by a Kyrodenian, named Aktalar Nesefer, approximately 1,000 years ago, for the sole purpose to siphon the magic power produced by genies. Hypothetically, one could use this to make a total of 18 wishes, or one wish that could affect the very universe itself. However, there was one aspect Aktalar did not count on."

"What's that?" I asked him.

"The unpredictable and mischievous nature of genies," he answered.

"What?" I said confused.

"See everyone expects genies to be submissive little play things," Stonegrave explained, "But the fact of the matter is, genies are deceptive, un-trust worthy, vile, and mischievous spiritual beings."

"That's not true," I tried to explain, "That can't be true."

"Sir Wilhelm," he replied, "We have a whole section in our library about the deceptive nature of genies. One ferret named Craven son of Ral, found a genie and wished to be king of the world. The genie transported him to a cruise ship, which immediately hit an iceberg and started sinking. He wished he was far away from the ship. Next thing he knew, he was falling down a cliff. Finally, he wished he was somewhere safe, the genie granted his wish by placing him in the prison cell in the Woodland Kingdom."

"Another poor fellow, Mentwell son of Zinn, unearthed a genie, and wished to be the most popular creature in the Valley. He did become poplar, but popular with bounty hunters. He was the most wanted outlaw in the Valley. He wished the bounty hunters to stop chasing him, which they did, but that didn't stop the sheriffs from running him down. He then wished for the sheriffs to stop chasing him, and they did, but he was back to where he was before he discovered the genie.

"Next, a rabbit named Jethro found a genie, and he wished to be the richest creature who ever lived. The genie granted his wish by supplying him with all the gold in the Valley. Unfortunately, the treasures were stolen from every single kingdom in existence. Once word got around that he was the one who had stolen all the treasure, he wished it all away. But he wasn't specific enough and the treasures did not return to their respected kingdoms, until he used his final wish to do so.

"There are a hundred more cases like it, but I know I've made my point quite clear. Genies are little devils, that cannot be trusted."

I was enraged, even though I could understand where he was coming from. How could he casually say this with the five ladies being in the same room?

"But Helina protected me," I protested, "She saved my life."

"Yes, because she had to," Stonegrave reminded me, "Whether she cared about you or not, she is obligated to protect your life."

I was about to say something but Helina spoke up.

"So, what you're telling me is that, I didn't have to grant my master's wish down to the letter?" she asked tremoring.

"Exactly," Stonegrave replied.

"Then, then, oh no!" she said slamming herself against the wall of her diamond.

"You put on quite an act miss," Stonegrave said eyeing Helina suspiciously.

"Shut up!" I shouted to him, "I know Helina, not once did she give me a reason to distrust her."

"Probably because she wants you to trust her," he said,

"I'm sorry brother, but Stonegrave is usually right about these things," my brother interrupted. "If this has been going on for centuries, then what's to say it won't happen again. At least now we know that this, Dhirkullah fellow will never get what he wants even if he does collect the final emerald."

"You don't understand," I told him, I went to grab Helina's diamond before Stonegrave stood in my way.

"I'm sorry Sir Wilhelm," he said, "I can't let you take it. She's Blue Wall property now, and plus I don't want her to deceive you even further."

*Property?* Was I hearing him right? I ran past him and grabbed Helina's emerald in a flash. I then made a mad dash out of there.

"Stop him!" Stonegrave said to his team.

"Don't," I heard my brother say.

Dhikrullah was never going to complete the set, if Helina and I would be on the run together forever.

"I thought you were tired of running?" Helina asked me.

"We're leaving Helina," I told her. "You and me together. So long Blue Wall, goodbye Rulksferd, see you around, kids? Oh, what am I doing?"

"Not thinking clearly, obviously," Helina remarked.

"It's better than listening to him lie like that," I told her. I was practically sliding down the hallway.

"You're going to abandon everything and everyone, just because some guy said something that ticked you off?" Helina pointed out. "I get it. Genies are always up to no good; they're always one step ahead."

"You're not like those genies," I answered her. I looked around. The hallways were so confusing: they were too similar to one another.

"Maybe that's because I suck at being one," Helina said, making me stop in my tracks. "I'm the worst genie that ever lived. Just think, Wilhelm, I didn't have to enslave an entire town, I didn't have to follow his wishes to the very letter, and the reason we're all in this mess is because of me."

"Nobody told you how to be a genie," I told her.

"It sure would have saved everyone a lot of trouble," she said under her breath.

With nothing else to say, I decided to take a look at which corridor we were in. The only thing distinguishable, was the giant tapestry hanging on the wall. My eyes followed the tapestry as the epic tale unfolded.

From what I could gather, it was an episode of the life of Melvin the Warrior. He was red from tail to ear, the common appearance for a red-eared squirrel. It depicted Melvin, locked up in a prison, by some evil king. The tapestry showed how Melvin dug under his cell with his bare claws to reach freedom.

"That was smart of him," I said out-loud, "Even though he was in a sticky situation he found a way out of it."

"Yeah," Helina mumbled in response.

"Say, there still might be a way out of this," I told her, "Just look how we got here. When we were facing the giant boar, did we mope around in pity?"

"No," the genie replied, "We looked for a way to bring him down, and now he's stuck in a lamp."

"Exactly," I said, "If I could face him despite being the worst ruler in history, and you could face him being the worst genie in history, who's to say we can't face Dhikrullah and his goons?"

"You're right," Helina replied, "Wait, you are right! What are we doing here? Let's find a way to take him down!"

"That's the spirit," I told her. I turned around, only to see plenty of hallways to choose from.

"Now only one thing stands in our way," I told her.

"Yeah, what?" Helina asked me.

"How do we get out of here?" I said with a gulp.

# CHAPTER XV

"Alright," I said to my brother and Stonegrave, "How can we free the genies from their diamonds?"

"Well it's quite simple really," Stonegrave explained, "The only way for the genies to escape the Ynjusay, is when the wish, or wishes, has been granted."

"So, it has to be used in order for the genies to be released," I said.

"Isn't that what I just said?" Stonegrave asked annoyed. "Anyway, unless you have the last diamond, the Ynjusay will have no use."

"Great," I exclaimed wanting to pound my paws on the podium, "How do we find it?"

"There is no way," Stonegrave said being blunt. "Unless it has been kept secret, or there's a document about where the last emerald is, it will be like looking for a needle in a hay stack, as the saying goes. Well, for all we know it could be on the other side of The Valley or in our backyard."

"Wait," my brother said, finally speaking for what seemed like a while, "There is one way."

"What's that?" I asked him. I admit it was rude, but I was kind of impatient.

"The sword of Melvin the Warrior," my brother announced, "The sword was magical itself you see. It was found in a cave on the coastlines near Lavash, the village where Melvin grew up. For centuries, it was stuck in a rock, waiting to be used by a true hero of honor. Many tried to release it from its resting place, but all failed to do so, except for Melvin. Only a magical sword, chooses its owner."

"How will it help us?" I asked him.

"Magical items seem to sense the presence of others," my brother explained, "Since the sword is magical, and the diamond is magical, then Melvin's sword could lead you directly to the final diamond."

"Sweet!" I exclaimed.

"Sweet, indeed," Stonegrave said in a monotone voice, "If someone could find the sword."

I looked at him confused.

"Upon Melvin's request, the sword was buried underneath the Abbey," he exclaimed. "He said the sword wanted to wait for the right hero to return. The only clue he instructed the monks to leave was something of a mystery. *You are that.* If it sounds familiar, it should be. It's the phrase written directly above Melvin's full body portrait on the tapestry."

"So, we can't find the diamond unless we get the sword," I said taking it all in, "And we can't get the sword, unless we figure out what *You are that* means?"

"Again, didn't I just say that?" Stonegrave asked more annoyed than ever.

\*\*\*

The rest of the day passed away, and I pondered like crazy. My brother thought another feast would be in order to lighten the spirits. I tried to be social, but those four words bashed themselves through my skull. Who knew that four simple words could cause a major headache.

I got out of my chair and excused myself for the night. As I walked down the hallway the words spun around my head, like a merry-go-round.

I looked back at the tapestry. Melvin was standing in full set of armor, with the four words "You are that" hovering above him

"What do you mean?" I shouted at it, not expecting an answer from it, but it would have been cool if it did.

I stood there just looking at him, holding his sword to the ground.

"The answer to what?" I heard a voice ask. For a second, I thought Melvin the Warrior had answered, until I noticed Timmore walking out of the darkness.

"That phrase," I said pointing to the blue words. Timmore squinted his eyes, and began mouthing the words as he read it.

"What an odd phrase," he remarked, "*You are that,* sounds like it doesn't mean anything."

"It's deceptive that way," I told him. "He wanted that exact phrase for a reason, I just have to figure out why."

We both stared at the words, continuing to ponder what they meant. But my eyes soon grew weary. My mind and body couldn't take it anymore.

"Well," I said giving my limbs a much-needed stretch, "Maybe a good night's rest will help. Good night."

"Good night, Sir Wilhelm," Timmore said still looking at Melvin's portrait.

"Hey," I said putting my paws on his shoulders, "Don't stress about it. We'll figure it out sooner or later."

"Are you sure?" Timmore asked now looking at me.

"I'm sure," I told him, "Let's give it a rest for tonight, okay?"

"Okay," Timmore replied, relaxing the muscles in his forehead.

\*\*\*

My bed chamber doors were slammed opened. It was morning, and Timmore and Rathaetouy had practically barged into my room.

"Sir Wilhelm," I heard Timmore exclaimed, "I figured it out; I know what it means!"

"What does what mean?" I asked half asleep.

"*You are that,* I know what it means now!" he said with excitement.

"What does it mean?" I asked him slowly becoming more alert.

"Well, my friends and I were playing this game. One of us would take a word, and scramble it up.

Whoever figured out what the word really was would win.

"You did the same with *You are that?*"

"Exactly! After many tries, I finally got all the letters together to make: *Rathaetouy*!"

My mouth dropped to the floor with amazement.

"I know how you feel," Rathaetouy said to me. "I didn't believe it myself, but after seeing it, I was surprised just as you are now."

"Great," I said filling with excitement, "But what now?"

"Well now, we're closer to Melvin's Sword," said Rathaetouy. "All we have to do now is figure out how my name will help us find the sword. I am so thankful for you, Sir Wilhelm. Without you, I wouldn't be as close to my destiny as I am now."

"But we have no idea what your name has to do with anything," I reasoned.

"We might have a clue," Timmore answered. "You know how the hallways are given a letter? Well, maybe each hallway has a clue to where Melvin's Sword is."

"It seems like you two have figured it out," I told to them. "What do you need me for?"

"It's only fair since you want to find it," Timmore answered.

"Alright," I said finally out of bed, "Let's find ourselves a sword."

We saw it best to start at the R Hallway.

Finding the hallway was the easy part, the hard part was trying to find a clue, a sign, a button, a lever or a loose brick.

"There must be something here somewhere," Rathaetouy said.

I was looking at a beautiful painting of a waterfall, when I saw a small *R* under the frame.

Rathaetouy pushed me out of the way, and pressed the *R,* which *caved* into the wall. The sound of clicks could be heard within.

"Good show," Rathaetouy said taking a deep breath, "On to Hallway A!"

Hallway A was near the main lobby of the abbey. The entrance door leading outside was large enough for pine trees to walk in, if the day ever came, and the doors were so thick they probably took ten or twenty animals to close them shut.

Aware of what to look for, Rathaetouy, Timmore, and I searched for an *A*.

*What is this, alphabet scavenger hunt?* I thought, amusing myself. It wasn't long until Timmore found a small *A* imbedded into the brick lying on the left corner of the hallway.

"Wait, there are two A's in Rathaetouy's name," I said in realization, "How do we know there are not two *A's* here? And if so, how do we know this is the right one?"

"We've searched the room from top to bottom," Rathaetouy commented, "This is the only *A* here."

"Let's search again," I said, "Maybe there's a second *A* somewhere around here."

Rathaetouy gave a small grunt

"What did I tell you?" Rathaetouy said annoyed when we had finished a second search. "That's the only *A* there, then that is the only *A* there."

Rathaetouy lunged himself ahead of Timmore and pressed down on it. Nothing happened.

"Maybe if I press it again..." Rathaetouy was about to say.

"No, maybe we have to come back after pressing on *T, H and E.*" I suggested.

"Don't be ridiculous," he chirped, "We'll have to come back after pressing *T, H* and E."

"Is there an echo in here? I just said that." I said confused.

"No time to feel sorry you didn't come up with it first," he replied, "Let's go!"

We approached the *T* hallway, which was one of the most beautiful hallways in Blue Wall Abbey. If I wasn't on the prowl for letters, I would have stopped and taken it all in for hours at a time.

A guard stood by two giant locked doors, and informed us the banquet room was being cleaned, and we weren't allowed inside.

Hanging above the door was a golden figure of a mythological creature named the bat. It was described as having pointy ears, and could walk like you or me, but it also had wings so it could fly. Back at Rulksferd, I heard some of my subjects telling stories of such a creature, but I never saw one up close and personal. One argument that claimed seeing one was a bad omen, while another argument stated the exact opposite. I didn't buy into them, but it was nice to ponder their existence now and again. But if genies were real, was it possible bats could be real too?

Real or not, bad or good, the attention to detail on the golden statue was fascinating, it almost looked like it could have sprung to life with a blink of an eye.

"What are you looking at Wilhelm?" Rathaetouy demanded, "Get looking for the *T*."

*Alright, alright, don't get your tail twisted in a knot* I wanted to say but never did. We must have looked like a bunch of idiots in front of the guard, but he was probably too polite to say anything.

We searched high and low, until Rathaetouy found a small golden *T* on the left railing. He pressed and again nothing happened, but we were already on our way to find Hallway H to not be worried about it.

Hallway H was next to the garden, and I found the *H* hidden by a specifically placed pot with symbols from a time long ago. We rushed back to Hallway A, and pressed the letter *A* again. This time it gave off the mechanical noise that we had become familiar with.

We went up the stairs to Hallway E and Timmore found the letter *E* next to an open door. I had to take a break after running down the stairs.

"Wait!" I screamed. "I'm not as young as you."

A few minutes later we arrived back at Hallway T and pressed letter *T*.

In the O Hallway, we found the *O* next to the hall's entrance. In the U Hallway, which was near the children's bed chambers, Rathaetouy found the *U* on a window railing. The kids stopped their games, once they heard the clicking and clunking inside the walls.

"What are you guys doing?" Berry asked for the group.

"We're looking for letters that's all," Rathaetouy announced, without giving me time to explain.

"Why?" asked Timothy II.

"Because they're..." Rathaetouy was about to answerer.

"We need them to find Melvin's Sword," I said butting in, Rathaetouy gave me a dirty look. "We need to find the sword because it will help us find the last diamond so we can stop Dhikrullah and his goons."

"But your pirate brother left them stranded on a deserted island," Berry pointed out.

"But when we have the last emerald," I explained, "We'll be ready for him. Okay?"

The kids didn't say anything for a little while until Robert asked, "Can we help?"

I could hear Rathaetouy's voice saying "no" but I beat him with my enthusiastic "yes" without a second to spare. The kids cheered in response.

"What letter should we look for next?" Berry asked.

"The letter *Y*," I informed them.

They all began to mutter to themselves, searching up and down for the letter *Y*.

"Not like that," Rathaetouy scoffed. "We have to find it in the *Y Hallway*."

The kids were about to run in every direction before Billy asked Rathaetouy where the Y Hallway actually was.

"Follow me!" he said turning around.

Finally, we arrived at Hallway Y, and everybody got to work on finding the *Y*. The walls were covered with the tapestry of Greyjoy the Strong.

"Brother Wilhelm," my brother said announcing his presence, "What on earth is going on here?"

"We're looking for Melvin's Sword," I stated.

"I tried to tell the kids to stay out of it," Rathaetouy explained, "But your brother thought it was good idea for them to tag along."

"Never mind that now," my brother said, stopping me from making a remark, "I don't think today is the right time to go looking for it."

"Why not? We just have to find one more. . ." Rathaetouy was about to say when we heard Samuel I exclaim, "Found it!"

I learned later that he found the letter *Y* behind the tapestry, for I could not at the time see where he discovered it. The gears made their presence known by making tons of clanks and clonks. From a short glance, my brother's face was covered with dread.

The floor began to shake as if the entire Abby was about to collapse on top of us. The tremors stopped as soon as they began, leaving the entire Abby as quite as a graveyard.

"What the what was that?" Berry asked breaking the silence.

My brother gave a long sigh before saying, "Follow me, I'll show you all."

I had not seen my brother so depressed since what seemed in forever. His head drooped down, and he walked at a snail's pace. My eyes scanned the area as we walked, wondering how there were no cracks in the walls or broken objects lying on the floor.

We arrived in the room with Melvin the Warrior's tapestry. It all seemed the same, except for the giant square hole next to Melvin's portrait. Upon closer inspection, there were stairs going down into a pit of darkness that not even the sunlight could pierce. Monks, servants, and other children who did not aide in the search entered the room to see what the commotion was about.

"Father Wilhelm," said Stonegrave, "I thought we all agreed that. . ."

"Not now Stonegrave," my brother said shutting him up.

"Get me a lit torch," Rathaetouy demanded with his paws shaking with anticipation. An abbey child scurried away, and came back with a lit torch and handed it to Rathaetouy.

With one deep breath, Rathaetouy took his first step into the black hole.

"Wait," my brother pleaded, "You don't have to go now. Melvin would have wanted you to be ready."

Rathaetouy turned his head and said, "Father Wilhelm, remember when we first met? My house was burned down, my parents were taken away from me, and I was alone with no one for help. I thought I was the unluckiest child in the whole world. But then you found me, and you told me that you had been looking for me. You told me I was the grandson of a great warrior; and the raid was meant to be. How else could you have found me? Where would Blue Wall Abbey be, if you didn't find me?"

"Rathaetouy, please you have to understand," my brother said about to tear up.

"I understand completely," Rathaetouy replied. "Your pirate of a brother, brought Sir Wilhelm and Timmore here. Can't you see? This was meant to be. It is my destiny; this is how I'm supposed to get Melvin's sword. If the stars have been aligned right now, the fates know that I'm ready."

"Very well," my brother said choking up, "It's just that, you will face many trials down there. I just can't imagine you getting hurt."

My brother gave Rathaetouy a hug.

"Whatever happens," my brother said tearing up, "Know that I am not the bad guy. All I've ever done was for you."

"Father Wilhelm, I'm grateful for you," Rathaetouy assure. "Don't worry; I'm the chosen one. I'll come out fine."

My brother and Rathaetouy released their embrace. As Rathaetouy walked down the steps, my brother slowly backed away.

"This is not a farewell," Rathaetouy said turning around, facing us, "When I come back, I'll have Melvin's Sword within my paws!"

With that, Rathaetouy continued his journey. The floor soon blocked any view of him, and his torch light slowly died out.

# CHAPTER XVI

"Alright," my brother said clasping his paws together, "Listen up everyone, and listen well. Rathaetouy will be facing many trials down there. You will hear screams, tears and probably words that don't make any sense. Do not pay heed to any of it. It will just be the stress of the trials. We're going to have guards at this spot, two for every shift. This is just a precaution, nothing to worry about, understand?"

The crowd nodded their heads, some said "Yes, Father" or "Understood."

"Now on to your daily routine," my brother continued, "All of you."

Everyone started to disperse and talked amongst themselves.

"Brother, Timmore," I heard my brother say to us, "Come with me."

He took off with a huff. I noticed how all the other monks started to walk in the same direction my brother was going.

"What's going on?" I asked, "What do you got locked down there?"

"All in good time," he answered.

I wanted to ask him more, until I heard something churning. I looked back, to see the hole being covered up by a tile. Could the monks have opened and closed it at will? If so, what was the point of the big scavenger hunt? Why didn't my brother do it the moment we talked about Melvin's Sword?

A line of monks flowed into one door. When Timmore and I passed through the arch, my brother closed the door behind us.

We were in some type of lecture room. We turned around to see a podium, and a line of chairs shadowing behind it. Lying in the center of the room were two chairs behind a table. The monks took their seats, and my brother sat behind the podium.

"Where do Timmore and I sit?" I asked him.

"Right there," my brother replied pointing to the two chairs behind the table.

"What's going on here?" I asked refusing to take my seat.

"Nothing," my brother answered calmly, "It's just a precaution, that's all."

"A precaution? A precaution against what?" I asked.

"You might have ruined everything!" Stonegrave said vaguely, "Six years of progress down the drain."

"Now Stonegrave control your temper," my brother said to him.

"What's going on brother?" I asked sincerely.

"Rathaetouy was never meant to find the sword," my brother explained. Brother Montague stood up and began to speak.

"Melvin was the first warrior of Blue Wall Abbey, and it became hard to find an animal worthy to replace him when he died. At first, we didn't know what to do, until we figured out a way that has worked for four generations."

"And you just had to mess it all up," Stonegrave interrupted.

"Order," my brother shouted at him, "You will speak when it is your turn. Montague please continues."

Stonegrave gave a small huff under his breath.

"Traditionally, the Father Abbot would pick one of the Abbey children that showed promise, and raise him or her as the chosen one," Montague said as if Stonegrave had barely utter a word, "We would tell the tapestry artist to change the words above Melvin to fit the letters of the chosen child's name. The child would be sent a way, so the engineers could change the gears within the walls depending on the letters. It was all a safeguard you see. We would tell the child they would one day discover Melvin's Sword. It was meant to take half their life to figure out the true arrangement of the letters, and the other half to figure out the connection between the letters and the hallways. But they would always figure out when they were too old to do anything about it. And so, it has worked, until now."

"Thank you, Brother Montague," said my brother as the frail mouse sat back down.

"But why tell them about the sword if they were never meant to find it?" Timmore asked reluctantly.

"It was something they would strive for," Stonegrave answered, "When they would figure the reason why the sword was not in their paws because they were unworthy, worthy, therefore, they would strive to be stronger, which would in turn give them the strength to protect the abbey."

"Thank you Stonegrave," my brother said turning his head again back at Stonegrave, "But from now on I'll be answering the questions from now on."

"But why all this?" I asked the group, "For all you know the sword might choose Rathaetouy, making this whole thing pointless."

"For one," my brother explained shushing Stonegrave, "What if it doesn't? Rathaetouy will surely come to realize this was a big charade. What then? You've probably put all our lives, and this abbey into jeopardy."

"What about the rest of the world?" I asked him.

"What do you mean?" he said confused.

"You know, and you know too Stonegrave, that we need that sword," I accused, "So that I can't find the last diamond, in order to defeat Dhikrullah who wants to mold the entire world into his image."

I heard Stonegrave give a little chuckle.

"You find that funny, Stonegrave?" I asked him.

"Quiet, coward," Stonegrave muttered. "Your brother told me everything I needed to know. Why so interested in saving the world? You need a boost to your ego? Be loved by everyone? You're already loved by the childern; that's not enough? No, it's never enough. I know where you're coming from."

I glared at him. If my claws weren't digging into the table, I don't know what I would have done.

"I'll let you in on a little secret," he continued. "Any magical item would have worked just as well as the sword. You could have taken the diamonds if you'd wanted. Me and your brother had our suspicions. To protect the world from you, we had to make you think that only the sword could track the last diamond down. I'm surprised you didn't think it odd when your brother said all magical items sense each other, but then I said the sword could only find the diamond, all while we were standing in a room filled with magical items."

How could I have been so foolish?

"Brother, how could you?" I said in disbelief.

"Brother Wilhelm," he said beginning to tear up again, "You have to believe me, I'm not the bad guy here. I, we, as a group, did what we thought was best."

I tried to put myself in his shoes, like what Helina said while on *The Executioner*.

"I get," I said taking a deep breath, "I understand. You don't trust me. You store just about every magical item in the Valley. It's your duty to make sure they don't fall into the wrong paws. I come here, out of the blew, with a magical item that could affect space and time. You want to know why I want to put a stop to this random creature named Dhikrullah?"

"Precisely," my brother said.

"Well, all you had to do was ask," I began. "The reason why I want to stop him, is that maybe, I can be forgiven. When I was in the cave, I realized I messed up; I ruined the family name, placed innocent creatures behind bars, and I just left them not caring if they would live to see the next day or not."

"On the island, I had quit feeling sorry for myself, and figured if I could save the world, maybe it would outweigh all the terrible things I had done. Everyone would forget the tyranny of Wilhelm IV. I would no longer have to deal with my rotten past and remake myself as the creature I know I should be. Satisfied?"

The silence allowed me to catch my breath.

"I'm sorry brother," my brother said, "But as Father of Blue Wall Abbey, I cannot and will not allow you to find the last diamond. Now, we will have to decide what to do with you."

"Are you all mad?" Timmore asked. The question startled not only the group of monks and me, but also Timmore himself.

"I've been with Wilhelm longer than any of you," he continued. "He is not the villain you think he is. He has shown nothing but kindness to us kids, and has tried his best to keep us out of harms way."

"But we can't trust you as well," Stonegrave commented. "When was the last the time magical items were stolen by loved ones with a sad story?" he asked the group.

"What is it with you Stonegrave?" I asked him. "First all genies are evil little beings, and the next all loved ones who have claimed to go through terrible trials are thieves?"

"If you were a monk here at Blue Abbey, you would know," Stonegrave said glaring at me. "You would know that nothing really changes. Selfish creatures remain selfish, thieves are still thieves, liars are still liars, and no matter how many chances you give them, they are bound to go back to the way they were before."

"I thought that's why you guys became monks in the first place," I uttered. "You were unhappy where your lives were going, so you changed course. Now I ask you Stonegrave, are your thieves still thieves, are your liars still liars?"

"That's enough!" he exclaimed. "You will not question the integrity of our brothers."

"But yet it's alright to question my integrity?" I pointed out.

"I am convinced Father Wilhelm, that your brother is deceiving us all," Stonegrave announced, "And he, and his accomplices, should be locked in the prison before he seduces the entire Abby."

"Thank you for your consideration Brother Stonegrave," said my brother politely, "But, I do not see it wise to imprison my brother when he hasn't committed any crimes against the Abbey's Code. Can you imagine the uproar if word got out?"

Stonegrave sulked into his chair.

"Therefore," my brother went on, "I am sorry, Wilhelm, but in order to make sure nothing like this happens again, I order you to leave by noon tomorrow. Court is now adjured."

With that he slammed a small mallet on his podium, and all the monks, who barely had any say in the matter walked out of the room. Stonegrave was the last monk to leave, before my brother came down from the podium and talked to us.

"Again, I'm dreadfully sorry," he said to us, "But it was the only way to bring peace back to our walls. How about we have a parting feast tonight?"

"Okay," I said. If only a feast could have solved everything.

# CHAPTER XVII

The musical instruments played their gleeful tunes, as the other two nights, but to me they hardly meant anything to my ears anymore. The adults cackled while the kids played together. They would not have been so merry if they were in the court room with me. If they had only seen what the monks really thought, or how the monks really operated things. I wanted to stop the festivities and tell them everything that I knew, but I did not wish to offend the monks even more.

Timmore told the boys that we would be leaving the next day and nothing more. As for me, I told Helina everything.

"I'm sorry Helina," I said to her. "I wish I could take you with me, but that would only prove Stonegrave right."

"I hate the idea of being left behind," Helina began, "But I believe one day you'll come back with the final diamond, and this whole thing will be done with."

"I also believed one day I would be free," said Maxine in her parched voice.

"Do you mind?" Helina asked her scouring, "I believe in you Wilhelm, you haven't come this far for nothing. I'm sure of it."

After saying goodbye to Helina, I returned to the feast. It all came to a halt when a guard came rushing toward us and began shouting, "Stop the music! Stop everything!"

The sound of merriment sank with the scared expression on the guard's face.

"What is it Sir Travestove?" my brother asked.

"We're surrounded on the water front," he announced. "Some sort of armada, they're coming in at a rapid rate."

"Are they the ships of the Oppentums?" my brother asked.

"No, they're none like we've ever seen before," Travestone wheezed. "They're sails are like spikes, and they're ships are pointed like swords."

"Those are Dhikrullah's ships," I said.

"More trouble from this Wilhelm fellow?" Stonegrave said finishing a glass of ale, "I knew it. Who's to say he's not in cahoots with them?"

"Brother Stonegrave," my brother said harshly, "Now is not the place, nor time. Alright everyone you know what to do. Ladies, children, and those who are too old or weak, head for lower levels. Those who know how to fire an arrow or are strong enough to fight, follow Brother Julius."

Everyone immediately got out of their seats in a rush. The fire was put out with one big splash of water.

"Come with me Wilhelm," my brother said.

"But for all you know I could betray you and hand you over to the enemy," I commented.

"I am not Stonegrave," he replied, "Again, come with me."

I reluctantly followed my brother. We walked up the steps inside a watch tower facing the dock. The first thing that caught my attention was the drumming sound that I was way too familiar with. There were about twenty or forty of Dhirkulla's ships heading towards the dock. I looked around to see other creatures holding bows in their paws.

"Do you know how to use a bow and arrow?" my brother asked suddenly.

"Wait, what?" I said raising my eyebrows.

"Do you know how to use a bow and arrow, yes or no?" my brother repeated.

"I've only used a wooden sword once," I informed him.

My brother looked around, grabbed a packet of arrows, threw them into my paws, and picked up the bow.

"Okay, it's pretty simple," he said demonstrating. "You hold the bow like this, place the arrow like this, pull back, aim, then release, got it?"

"Got it," knowing I should have said no.

"Alright, don't worry I'll be shooting right beside you," he said with confidence. The larger ship was closing in fast, while creatures on the dock started running towards the entrance before it was closed.

"Steady men," my brother order, "Wait for them to strike first."

The more I watched, the more I realized that I was not supposed to be here. I could have protected the kids or made sure that everyone was safe in wherever they placed the unfit creatures.

The larger ship began to dock in an empty space. The vicious passengers came out and started making their way towards us.

"Why good evening gentle creatures," I heard Dhikrullah say. "You have something of ours. Give it to us, and we'll leave in peace."

"You're going to have to be more specific" my brother yelled back.

"You know what I mean," Dhikrullah said. "Just give it to us, and we'll leave you be."

"Even if we do have what you want, which we don't, as property of Blue Wall Abbey, we will not give it away to some sea rats," my brother yelled back.

"Well if that's the way you want it," Dhikrullah said before one of his man blew an obnoxious blast from his horn.

"Get ready men," my brother ordered.

The ships came closer, and before I knew it the sky became littered with flames. Most of the arrows hit the base of the wall, while one of our archers was hit.

My fur turned pale as the archer's fur burnt up. The poor fellow hit the ground with a thud.

"Fire at will!" my brother shouted.

Archers all around me started firing at the ships, while others aimed for Dhikrullah and his army.

It was the moment of truth for me. I picked an arrow, placed it in my bow, aimed at a ship, and fired. The arrow fell straight down like a boneless chicken. I took another arrow, placed it in my bow, aimed at the same ship, pulled back and fired. The arrow almost skinned my paw. I looked at my brother and he was releasing arrows by the second.

The flames, next to the wall, were growing at a rapid rate. Some arrows landed in the festivities area, catching the grass on fire. It feltlike I was the only one who saw the hopelessness of the situation. Nothing was working.

"Wilhelm what are you doing?" my brother asked angrily, "Shoot like your life is on the line. Your life IS on the line."

I shot a third time; the arrow went straight down to the ground. Fourth time, the arrow somehow went shooting in the sky, and I wasn't even pointing my bow in that direction. Fifth try, the arrow went flying through the air, in the opposite direction, and shattered a glass window.

More ships began to dock, whether there were enough open spaces or not.

"They're bringing out the ram!" someone exclaimed.

"Brace the gate!" my brother shouted.

"Brace the gate!" I heard someone shout from below.

One of Dhrikullah's ships dropped off pa few men holding up an angry looking ram. They stormed through the boardwalk and were heading straight to the gate.

"Shoot the ram!" someone shouted. I'm surprised I didn't lose my hearing, from the creatures shouting, arrows flying, fire cracking, and drums drumming. Two rodents ran up with a bucket of water and poured it onto the flames, before running back to the well to refill. I looked back once, only to see the grass being singed.

*BAM! BAM! BAM!*

"Shoot the ram! Goodness sakes shoot the ram!" someone shouted again.

I tried to aim for the ram, but I almost fell to my death looking for it. They were already under us, we were unable to shoot at them. If I couldn't stop the ram from breaking in, at least I could have tried to get as many goons as I could.

It looked like every enemy ship had unloaded, and a sea of black covered the board walk.

I aimed for their heads, and released an arrow for the seventh time, eighth time, and a ninth time.

"Brother, we need to retreat," I tried to reason with him.

"A good archer of the abbey never leaves his post!" he shouted back at me.

"That's the thing, I'm not a good archer," I said to him, but he completely ignored me.

An enemy arrow landed inches away from me, setting the platform on fire. I had to move unless I wanted to make an untimely death with the ground.

"We need to get going," I yelled at my brother.

"Just a few more minutes," he shouted back.

The wood underneath us gave way to the spreading flames. I flung my bow and pack full of arrows and pushed my brother towards the tower.

It happened in seconds, but to me everything was moving in hours, I could make out every detail. I could feel the impact between me and my brother. I remember the platform giving away. My feet were floating in the air, as the platform fell to the earth below.

I pushed my brother with such a force, that he flew into the entrance way and was an inch away from sliding down the stairs. I, however, was unable to reach the tower in time, hanging on the edge of the wall.

"Brother, help me," I begged for dear life. A couple of seconds letter, my brother grabbed me by the paw, and with all our strength, I was back on a stable surface.

"We need to get to the gate," my brother commanded, before taking off down the stairs.

Our paws were finally on solid ground, but nowhere near out of danger. Half of the monks in the abbey pushed against the gate as the flames grew in size. The square rose bushes became a skeleton of black sticks, while the marble statues glowed bright orange.

I glanced at my brother, who was taken aghast by all the destruction around him. He started mumbling to himself.

"We need to hide the magical objects," I finally heard him say under his breath, "We have to hide them."

He then took off. I was getting tired of following everyone. My brother rushed through two doors leading inside, but then the flames blocked my path.

*Well, I guess I'm on my own* I thought to myself. Outside of the abbey, the group of creatures were pushed against the gate; on the inside of the abbey, not a single flower was safe, and the path of pebbles might as well have been charcoal.

The smell of smoke became overwhelming. If you have never smelt smoke before, it is the worst kind. Unlike others, it burns your nostrils and clogs up your lungs like rocks and makes coughing pure torture. Enough whiffs could literally choke you to death. Smoke also makes your eyes turn into a waterfall, making it hard to see.

Pulling the fabric of my cloak over my mouth did away with the breathing problem, but the same was not so for my running eyes. I heard coughing, a child's coughing.

I scanned the area to see Timmore and Berry, clearly out of breath and exhausted from extinguishing flames, lying on the ground. I bolted for the two kids, and picked them both up with my strength. Who knew that two kids could weigh so much!

I high tailed it out there and headed for the first opening to indoors I saw. Timmore and Berry came to. "We have to put out the fire," Berry said weakly.

"Oh no, you're not," I told them.

"But what about the abbey?" Timmore asked.

"The abbey is lost now," I told him. "Let Dhikrullah deal with the flames."

We walked down the hallway together, feeling safe in the abbey walls.

"I wonder what Rathaetouy would do," Timmore pondered.

"Oh, my goodness!" I exclaimed, "Rathaetouy, I can't believe I've forgotten about him."

This was our chance to free Rathaetouy. Looking back on it now, we didn't have much of a plan, but it was all we had.

Running down the corridors and hallways, made me wonder why this giant place didn't have a map. Maybe I should have mapped it all out while looking for the sword.

Finally, we found the room where the tapestry of Melvin the Warrior hung with pride. To our luck the place was unguarded. I put my paws against the wall, hoping to find some trigger or button.

"What are you doing Sir Wilhelm?" asked Timmore.

"It has to be here somewhere," I said barely acknowledging the question. It was then when I found the button next to a lit torch. The same tile opened, revealing the same stairs leading downward.

"Wait," Berry said with his mouth agape, "All that time searching for the letters was pointless?"

I grabbed the lit torch, and placed my foot on the first step.

"I'm going in," I told them.

"I'm coming to," Timmore replied.

"We don't know what's down there," Berry pointed out.

"Rathaetouy is down there, and that's good enough for me," I reminded him. "You would rather be up here when Dhikrullah and his goons come in?"

"Good point," Berry said joining us.

With torch in paw, we walked down the stairs together, into the darkness.

# CHAPTER XVIII

The deeper we went, the less we heard from the outside world. It was nice to take a breather from all of the chaos above. It reminded me of being inside the cave, which seemed like years ago. They were both damp, cramped, and, obviously, pitch black dark. Yet this time, I had two kids following me, and I was relying on the light of a torch rather than the light of gold.

There were no carvings on the dirt walls, only cracks and roots. The further we walked, the closer both walls were near to each other. We even had to suck in our guts at one point to get through. Then the hallway of earth finally opened out, and we were in a big circular room with pictures and symbols carved on every wall.

In the middle of the room were four stairs leading up to a platform, with Melvin's sword standing in the center of the platform.

"Rathaetouy?" I said with enough courage to speak.

No answer.

Timmore and Berry walked around the platform before announcing at once, "Found him!"

I made my own way to the other side to see what they had discovered.

There he was lying on the floor fast asleep.

"Rathaetouy," I said trying to wake him up. "Rathaetouy!"

"Huh, what?" he mumbled while opening his eyes. "Why Sir Wilhelm, Timmore, and... you."

"It's Berry by the way," Berry informed him.

"Yes," Rathaetouy stretching his arms, "What are you guys doing down here. Why and how?"

"Blue Wall Abbey is being invaded," Timmore told him, "Remember that Dhikrullah guy I told you about? Well he's leading the invasion!"

"Oh, my goodness!" Rathaetouy exclaimed. He walked up the steps, and placed his paws on the hilt of the sword.

"Come on," he said, "Blue Wall Abbey needs me."

He took a break for a few seconds, before trying to lift the sword up again.

"Rathaetouy," I said cautiously, "I don't know how to put this, but. . . I'm afraid, it's not meant to be."

"Sir Wilhelm," he said, "If there was ever a time Blue Wall Abbey needed a hero with Melvin the Warrior's sword, it is now."

"That's not what I'm saying," I tried explaining it to him. "I mean you. are not the chosen one."

Rathaetouy stopped his struggle and gave me a good long look.

"Nice," he said unexpectedly after a long pause, "More of that, please."

"What?" I asked obviously confused.

"Keep telling me how bad I am, and it will motivate me to get the strength to pull the sword out."

"No, Rathaetouy, I'm not trying to motivate you. I'm being honest with you."

"There we go, some more, please."

"Listen, my brother lied to you."

"He would never lie to me. He's the Father of the Abbey and my mentor; he'd never lie to me."

"He lied because he wanted to make you feel better."

"Yes, just a bit more, and this puppy will be free at last."

"LISTEN TO ME RATHEATOUY!" I shouted, a little louder than I wanted it to. Timmore and Berry shrunk back, while Rathaetouy's ears plopped flat onto his face. My voice echoed from wall to wall and probably all the way back outside.

"Oh, my," Rathaetouy said after my voice faded, "You're . . .you're serious."

His paws let go of the hilt.

"But it's impossible," he told us while walking down the stairs in a daze, "I'm the chosen one of Blue Wall Abbey. I'm the grandson of Melvin the Warrior himself. I aced every class, I was the best student in archery, swordsmanship and everything I've ever done. Then you guys came here and showed me the way to Melvin's sword. How can I not be the chosen one?"

"We never meant to help you find his sword in the first place," Timmore said speaking up, "Sir Wilhelm's. . . Father Wilhelm led us to a room and told us everything; how it was his job, as Father Abbot, to choose a chosen one who would protect the abbey, tell the kid they're the chosen one and tell him about the sword so would have something to strive for. But never were the chosen ones meant to actually find Melvin's sword."

"No, I don't believe you," said Rathaetouy. "I get it. This place is playing with my mind, using my imagination against me. Well, it's not working."

Rathaetouy ran back to the sword, in hopes he could pull it out.

"Rathaetouy," I said feeling like I was repeating myself, "The sword chose Melvin the Warrior. If the sword wanted you as its owner, it would have slipped out already."

"La, la, la, I'm not listening," he said.

"Please," I begged him, "I'm sorry we're the ones to tell you. I'm sorry you have to find out this way, but it's the truth. You are not the chosen one."

"Lies, lies, lies," Rathaetouy said aggressively, "Father Wilhelm told me I would face trials, this must be one of them. I will prevail, I must. Father Wilhelm never lies. He's never lied. He always looked after me; he was there for me. He gave me a home, clothes, all the food I can eat, everything I've ever wanted. . . how dare you betray him! Wait, what if you're just a figment of my imagination? Then. . . never mind. Go away, your efforts are useless."

I didn't want to do it, but my temper got the best of me. I ran up the stairs in a huff, and pushed him out of the way.

"Can your imagination do that?" I asked catching my breath. "Put your paws over my mouth, does that air feel fake to you? Feel my cloak, you can't touch your imagination, can you?"

"This placed has bewitched me," Rathaetouy said in a frenzy. "The more I stay the more this place takes over my mind, soon I won't be able to tell the difference between reality and fantasy."

I placed my paws on his shoulders and looked directly into his eyes.

"Do I look real to you?" I asked him.

I could see his pupils dial back in shock.

"It can't be," he said getting his strength back, "But, Father Wilhelm wouldn't lie."

"He lied to me too," I told him.

"I-I-I don't get it," he said walking down the stairs. "Does that mean, I've wasted my life?"

"Hey, don't say that," I said encouragingly, "You're still young, it's not like you're not as old as Brother Montague."

I gave out a small chuckle, but Rathaetouy didn't see the humor.

"Hey look at this," we heard a gruff voice say from the outside, "These creatures sure are stupid, I thought you were supposed to hide a secret passage way, not leave it open for all to see."

"They were too easy to take down," a scrappy voice replied, "So, they probably are that stupid."

"Let's check it out," the gruff voice said, "Some of them might be stupid enough to actually be hiding in there."

"Did you bring any weapons?" I whispered to Rathaetouy, worried the two intruders would hear me.

"No, remember?" he whispered back.

We heard one of the intruders walk down the steps, before requesting a torch.

I gave a sigh a relief. At least we had a bit more time to plan what to do.

"Okay, we have two options," I explained, "One of us could try to get the sword out. The other one, is to be captured."

"The chances of the sword choosing one of us are a million to one," Berry reasoned.

"Well, we might as well try," I told him. "I'll go first."

I walked up the steps with haste. I put all I had into lifting the sword out. The blasted thing would not budge. Even though I was lifting up, I felt a force pushing me down. The more effort I put into lifting it, the stronger the mysterious force pushed.

"I'll go next," Berry said after I walked down the steps.

He tried pulling it out, but I could tell he was dealing with the same conundrum I had only seconds earlier.

Timmore's turn came up next.

"Hey you guys, paws where I can see them!" we heard the rough voice demand.

A skinny otter and a raccoon, both wearing black robes, pointed their thick, curved swords at us.

"Hey you, put down the sword," the skinny otter commanded.

Timmore was shocked to see, there in his paws, was Melvin's Sword! He released it from his grasp immediately. The sword only fell halfway before rising back into his paw.

"I told you to put down the sword!" the raccoon repeated slowly making his way towards Timmore.

"I'm trying to," Timmore said throwing the sword to the ground only for it to come back every time.

Our ears suddenly picked up the sound of mechanical gears coming to life.

"What's going on?" the raccoon asked with a little tremor in his voice.

At first it seemed like the walls were moving upward, when, in reality, the floor was tilting downwards. We all lost our footing, and tumbled down the slanted floor. The raccoon and otter tripped, and would have fallen with us if they had not grabbed on to the edge in time.

It wasn't long until we three were forced to the mercy of the air as we continued to fall. At long last we hit the ground with a thud, and there we laid, for a very long time.

# CHAPTER XIX

"Is everyone alright?" I asked struggling to pick myself back up. I looked around, we were outdoors, that much was certain. The chaos from last night dissolved into a peaceful morning, or was it afternoon?

All of my bones ached, and I was surprised that I could have survive such a fall. I gave out a sneeze, launching a blanket of dust from my clothes. Berry coughed violently in response and woke up with a painful groan.

"What happened?" he asked opening his eyelids.

"Anything broken Berry?" I asked coming to his aide.

"Hold on," Berry responded. He first moved his arms, his paws second, his neck third, and finally his knees. He moaned at every minute and soon replied with, "A few aches, but I don't feel like anything is broken."

I grabbed him by the paw, and I helped him get up. He gave out a painful yelp, but he quieted down once he got used to walking around again.

"Rathaetouy, Timmore?" we both shouted out hoping to find them.

"Ouch," I yelled. It was like I stubbed my paw against a stone, but when I looked down, there was Rathaetouy lying flat on his back.

I shook Rathaetouy with all my might calling out his name to wake him up.

"Oye," he said batting me away. At least his arms and paws were in working order. He rolled himself on the grass.

"I found Timmore," I heard Berry announce from afar. I helped Rathaetouy we both looked at the wall in front of us. From the side we were on, it was hard to believe all the chaos even happened.

Berry and Timmore walked towards us.

"What do we do now?" Berry spoke up .

"Well," I said making a smacking noise with my lips, "Since we have the sword now, we can just follow it to the last diamond."

"Alright," Berry said looking at Timmore. The sword stayed forcefully planted in his paws.

"Okay sword," he said to it, "Do your stuff."

He held the sword with both paws, pointed sideways below his chest, and moved in a perfect circle. Timmore moved the sword back and forth, as if trying to pick up the emerald's scent. Finally, he pointed the sword west and said, "I'm not sure if it's anything, but I think I'm feeling movement in the sword this way. It may be nothing since it's so weak, I don't really know."

"We have nothing to tell us you're wrong so far," I said. "Let's get moving."

We trudged through the forest, with no path in sight for miles. Throughout our journey, we just imagined a path with the large gaps that weren't covered by leaves, sticks, or trunks. I dare not touch anything. For all I knew, half of the plants could have been poisonous to the touch.

With no one speaking I hummed a few notes to a song one of the artist played in my courts.

"What are you humming?" Berry asked me.

"*The Greytaeils' Odyssey*," I answered.

"You sure do ask a lot of questions," Rathaetouy commented.

"It's the only way to be one step ahead," Berry replied. "Plus, it's the only way I learned anything."

"You should have been there when we served in Kharull's, or now Dhikrullah's army," Timmore piped in, "Berry used to ask me his question, because our chief commander was completely aggravated by them. Now he's smarter than me."

"To an extent," Berry said humbly, "I mean, we all have our short comings, including myself."

"Now I have a question for you *Master* Berry," I announced. "Do you see any plants safe to eat?"

Berry looked around and said, "Well those mushrooms right there look good. Usually the colorful ones are poisonous, other than that I'm not sure. I've heard maggots, and blue beetles are quite tasty though."

Rathaetouy gave out a gag, which Timmore found quite humorous.

"What is *The Greytaeils' Odyssey* about anyway?" Berry asked inquisitively.

"Well, I don't know how it goes exactly," I admitted.

"Come on Sir Wilhelm, sing for us," Timmore and Berry begged.

"Okay, okay," I told them, "But I warn you, I don't know all of the words, and my singing voice is a bit rusty."

"Just make the words up as you go along," Timmore encouraged, "Don't mind how good your singing voice is, it's just us and nobody else."

"Alright, here it goes," I said before taking a deep breath.

The song took place near a farm on the outskirts of Rulksferd. It was tended by a farmer, and his sons Greytaeils and Moleveil. While working in the fields, Greytaeils accidently killed his brother, by driving a hoe into his skull. Some romanticized violent details later, Greytaeils runs away in fear of punishment. On his travels, he meets a witch who tells him the only way to bring Moleveil back to life was to bring his soul back from the Underground.

His first task was to find an opening to the Underground world. The only way to do this was to seek the council from the bats. The bats didn't believe him unless he proved his worth. One strenuous task later, Graytaeils proved himself and the bats directed him to the nearest entrance to the world below.

In the Underground, Greytaeils fought off monsters, dragons and other creatures of that sort. Long story short, Graytaeils found his brother's soul and escaped to the outside world. Moleveil's soul was reunited with his body and all was forgiven.

"That was pointless," Rathaetouy commented, "All that work just to go back to the way things were?"

"Well it brightened up our souls, didn't it?" I pointed out, "After what we've faced last night, at least we can think of something nice. If there was hope for Greytaeils, then there's hope for us."

"But it was all made up," Rathaetouy argued, "Graytaeils, Moleveil, all of it, just a work of fiction."

"The song might have things that actually happened," Berry commented. "Who knows Graytaeils might have been a real farmer's boy, maybe his brother was on the verge of death, but somehow, he still lived."

"And I guess you'll say that bats once flew from one point of the Valley to the other," Rathaetouy said mockingly.

"For a while I believed magic didn't exist," I told Rathaetouy, "But then I found your abbey and it was chock full off. . ."

I had no time finish; a bright light came out of nowhere. When we opened our eyes, and there we saw him, Dhikrullah, wearing the silver slippers while holding the bottomless bag besides him.

"Well, well, well," Dhikrullah said with a grin, "Look who we have here."

Despite the grim situation, Rathaetouy, Berry and Timmore gave out a small chuckle.

"Sir Wilhelm look," Timmore whispered, "He's wearing high heels!"

"They are not high heels," Dhikrullah said offended. "They are slippers."

"That's a cute bow right there," Berry said brining the tiny bows on the strap to our attention.

"ENOUGH!" Dhikrullah said fed up with our immature humor, "I did not come here to be mocked. Thanks to those kind, and generous monks, I have my paws on the most magical items in the Valley."

"So, you have all the things you need," I said to him. "Why do you need the Ynjusay."

"Isn't it obvious?" he argued, "While these items affect the here and now, the Ynjusay affects time itself. These are just tools to get what I want."

"To kill us?" I asked him, "Is that what you want?"

He gave out a small chuckle and said, "While locked in that cage, all I could think about was killing you. But then I realized you wouldn't be around to bow before me as I took over the world. Same with you Timmore, and you Berry. Yes, I know your names. A good leader knows all the names of his subjects, young or old."

"What about me?" Rathaetouy asked, "Surely, you must have some plan for me."

"Maybe you'll be a special slave, I don't know I haven't figured out how you play a part in any of this, but I will sooner or later," Dhikrullah answered, "Now I believe we were looking for last the diamond, is that correct?"

"Why don't you have the Uru-guy handle it?" I asked him.

"Because I killed him," Dhikrullah said nonchalantly.

"What? Why?" I asked in shock.

"When I heard that only the Sword of Melvin could find magical items, I saw no point in having him around any longer," he answered, "So I made sure he was executed, before telling these slippers to take me to the one that holds Melvin's Sword."

*Was it possible that one of my brother's lies paid off?* I thought to myself.

Timmore looked at me, wondering if we should attack or surrender to Dhikrullah's wishes.

"Can we have a moment to talk this out amongst ourselves?" I asked hopefully.

"Shut up!" he said thrusting the wand at me like it was a spear, "I should turn you into bugs like you really are. Now get a move on."

We trudged along the forest, past a lake, a cabin, and tiny waterfall. I couldn't put my paw on it, but the scenery felt oddly familiar. It wasn't long, until my feet were hurting like crazy.

"It's getting stronger now," Timmore informed.

"Good," Dhikrullah said smiling, "That's what I want to hear."

"Is it just me or do I smell smoke?" Berry said sniffing every now and again.

None of the rest of us smelled anything of the sort. We thought maybe he was smelling the smoke from last night, but that didn't seem right. After what felt like hours and hours of walking, I just couldn't take it anymore.

"Dhikrullah," I said panting, "I know you think of me as scum, but can we at least take a break?"

"Seeing you all in pain is my pleasure," he said, "We keep walking until we find the last diamond, understand."

"Understood," I said while thinking the complete opposite.

Maybe it was the heat, the walk, the hunger, or all of the above that made me think that I could get Dhikrullah on our side if he knew the truth.

"Listen Dhikrullah, your highness," I said, probably under the delusion of the heat, the walk, the hunger or all of the above, "Kharull was not this god that you believe he was. He used a genie's magic to force you to follow him. Can't you see that you're under this spell? You just have to wake up, and realize how messed up this really is."

His paws froze in place, leading us to stop dead in our tracks. He turned around, grabbed a magic wand out of the bag, and menacingly pointed it at me.

"For all you know he could have taken your wife, girlfriend, sister, or daughter as one of his harem girls right under your snout." I continued, "Don't you see anything wrong with that?"

"My love for the Great Kharull is all I need. What more could I want? When I make my wish, you will know the glory of Kharull as much I do."

"Do you even remember your life before Kharull?"

"Yes, I was as young as these fellows are now. I was a son of a sandal maker, but when Kharull came into my village, I had incredible feelings I had never felt before."

"That was the genie's magic taking effect."

"After all I saw of him, not once did I see him use a genie. Everything he ever did was from his own power."

"How was he so great that you had to put everything down to follow him?"

Dhikrullah was silent for a long time, before saying, "I don't remember, but that's not the point."

"How could you not remember?" I asked him, "He must have done something so great you wanted to follow him."

"Shut up!" he said thrusting the wand at me like it was a spear, "Never talk again, unless I say so, understand."

"Sure," I said knowing there was no more I could do to reason him out of it.

We continued our trek through the woods, with the smell of smoke becoming stronger and stronger. The number of trees we saw were becoming less and less as the smell of charred wood took over our senses.

Once we passed a line of trees, all of us saw the horrifying sight. It was a place I knew all too well, not because I had been there before, but that I recognized the castle barely standing near the horizon; it was my castle, I was back in Rulksferd. It wouldn't be long until I learned my fears of Rudding's rule, were terrifyingly true.

# CHAPTER XX

The houses were on the verge of falling apart. Every shred of grass was covered in black soot, and the trees barely had any leaves left. What was most concerning was that I couldn't see any villagers roaming around anywhere.

"Where is everyone?" Timmore asked taking note.

"Who cares?" Dhikrullah stated, "It won't matter till we get the diamond."

Our feet crunched under the rumble. As we looked at each dilapidated house after the other, we noticed how even the backyard farms were deprived of life. Even some of the fences were lying on the ground.

The winds blew through the alleyways intensifying the unnerving atmosphere of the entire village. Granted, we barely had walked past the walls, but this village had to have more life than this. This made me even more afraid of the state of the castle.

We continued to think that we were the only animals in the entire area, until we heard a gruff voice exclaim, "Hey you there!"

It was a castle guard, decked out in battle armor, carrying a massive sword too tiny and bulky for his own paws.

"Hey, buddy," I said in response, "It's me, Wilhelm IV, long time no see."

"Yeah, nice one kid," he said sarcastically, "And I'm Murray son of Grinslock."

"I have no idea who that is," Timmore admitted.

"I can explain," said Rathaetouy. "Murray son of Grinslock was considered history's most..."

"Enough with this nonsense," Dhikrullah said cutting him off. "You son, kill him."

Both the guard's and Timmore's eyebrows raised with shock.

"Come on with it," Dhikrullah said impatiently. When he realized Timmore wouldn't follow his orders, Dhikrullah took out his wand, and waved it towards the guard.

The guard's pupils moved upward into his head, while his mouth opened completely and his tongue stuck out limp and lifeless. He made a blood curdling croaking sound from his throat, before collapsing to the ground with a great thud.

"Let's get a move on," Dhikrullah said nonchalantly.

"How did you do that?" I asked him terrified, avoiding to look at the mangled corpse.

"I just thought what I wanted, and I made it so." Dhikrullah replied.

It was then when I made plans to snatch the wand out of his paws, but each version concluded in failure.

A loud trumpet blast revealed our presence. The blast was followed by the sound of a stream of arrows flying our way. We braced for impact, all except for Dhikrullah. He used the wand to turn the arrows around, and sent them back where they had come from.

Despite the sign of terror and reluctance, Timmore continued to lead us to the castle. Suddenly, it hit me. Why didn't Dhikrullah use his I magical slippers to find the last diamond himself? Maybe Brother Stonegrave never told him or maybe Dhikrullah didn't care.

More knights came out, riding on horseback; Dhikrullah twiddled the wand again, bringing a blanket of confusion amongst the horses. One way or another, each knight hit the ground. Dhikrullah was ready for the knights to come our way. Two knights were made an example of his terror. Their legs were twisted, more than once, with each twist the cracking of bones could be heard.

The rest of us simply couldn't take it anymore.

"Stop it!" Timmore said, and to further his point he rooted his paws on the uneven path, "I'm not moving unless you agree to stop bringing pain upon these innocent creatures."

"Innocent?" Dhikrullah said appalled, "They're trying to kill us."

It was then when Dhikrullah pointed the wand at Timmore.

"No, Dhikrullah, stop it!" I said afraid for Timmore's life. He then pointed the wand at me, and to my horror, I couldn't move. I was frozen in place.

"Hmmm..." he said with a chuckle, "I think I like you this way. Now, where was I? Oh, yes, I remember."

With the flick of the wand, Dhikrullah lifted Timmore into the air, and forced the sword out of his paws.

"I should have done this a long time ago," Dhikrullah said as the sword floated into his own paws.

He grabbed the hilt of it, and a sizzling sound could be heard.

"Youch!" he screamed as he released the sword, the bag, and the wand. Timmore fell to the ground, the horses calmed down, and my body started with a jolt as I became unfrozen.

The sword flew into Timmore's paws, as it always did, I grabbed the wand out of Dhikrullah paws, and Rathaetouy grabbed the bag.

"Now you listen to me, Dhikrullah," Timmore said pointing the sword at him, "I have the chance to kill you right now."

"Stop right there," the other knights announced, avoiding their friends screaming in pain.

"You're our prisoner now," Timmore continued, "And what I say goes."

"You're under arrest by order of Emperor Gaheeto," the knights declared.

"Gaheeto?" I asked surprised. Gaheeto of Raven Dale, was my third cousin twice removed. . . or was he my second cousin thrice removed?

Questions filled my head like:

*Is Rulksferd an empire now?*

*How did Gaheeto become emperor?*

*Where did all these villagers come from?*

*What are we going to do?*

*What is Timmore going to do?*

*What is Dhikrullah going to do?*

"We surrender," Timmore putting his paws up. The four of us did the same. The villagers talked amongst themselves, as the knights put our paws through wooden slates with holes in them and tied our paws with rope. More knights came over. They picked up the bag, the wand, and they tried grabbing the sword, but the sword would not leave Timmore's side.

So, there we were, escorted to my castle, with our paws tied and bound, and with everyone watching.

# CHAPTER XXI

We were ushered through the hallways and corridors. Some of the carpets, tapestries, flags, and doors were damaged, but the castle itself was structurally intact.

Two guards stood by the destroyed entrance way to the throne room. The knights obstructed our view at first, but once we were fully in the room, we saw how much life moved on since my absence.

Gaheeto sat on the same giant throne I had once sat on, and the same crown that he wore was the same that had rested on my head. Who would be standing next to him, but Rudding himself. Gaheeto almost looked like me, except for his orange fur and blue eyes.

"Cousin Wilhelm!" Gaheeto said about to get up from his seat, "Which one are you? The fifth or fourth? Doesn't matter. Don't tell me you're in this mess."

The knight brought the charges against me and my friends.

"Do what you want with the rest, it's Wilhelm I'm interested in," Gaheeto commanded.

"Yes, my Lord," the knight said.

"No, wait Gaheeto, you don't understand," I begged him, as the knights pushed my friends away.

"Don't worry the knights aren't that bad," he said calmingly. "I'm sure they'll treat them with the upmost hospitality; now on to business."

"I won't talk unless I know that my company is not harmed," I demanded.

Gaheeto gave out a sigh, before giving out my order.

"Happy?" he asked me.

"Yes," I said.

"Now maybe we should get down to business?"

"We may,"

"So, why are you here, Wilhelm? Rudding said you were killed by the mob, and now you appear after we heard reports of an animal mutilating our knights. Where have you been all this time?"

"You'd be amazed: in a desert, in a cave, on an island, in a boat on the sea, in a pirate ship on the sea, in a monastery, and now here. Maybe I should write a book about it one day."

"Yes, one day, but what are you doing here now?"

Should I tell him about the magical items lay right next to me, or should I have make something up on the spot? Knowing Rudding, he would use them for harm rather than for goodwill.

"Thought I'd come back to see how Rulksferd was doing," I answered.

"Well are you pleased with what you see?" Rudding asked me, "Because of your act of tyranny, Rulksferd is now in an even worse state than it was before you left. Is that what you came to see, the consequences of your actions? It was a nightmare that we had to deal with, but we've got the job done."

"So, that destruction outside, was my fault?" I said with a gulp.

"Precisely," Rudding confirmed, "What, did you think that was your cousins fault? What did I tell you Gaheeto? Wilhelm never thought about others only himself."

"I know Rudding, you and the citizens of this Empire have told me time and time again," Gaheeto said speaking up, "But who were those characters with you, and that other one who killed one of our best men?"

"He's trying to take over the empire," Rudding said, assured in his assumption. "He probably swindled those three children and hired that guy to kill you so that he could retake his place of the ruler of Rulksferd. If I were you I would put him in prison and sentence him to death!"

"Wait, no, Gaheeto, that's not why I came at all," I said.

"Then why are you here?" Rudding asked for him.

I was at a loss for words, what could I say? If I had told the truth, they would be tearing each other apart over the magical items.

"I can't tell you," I said making a compromise.

"I see," Rudding said with the face of victory.

Gaheeto tapped his paws on the arm rest of the throne.

"I have a better idea," he said at once, "Until you tell us what your business is here in Rulksferd, I sentence you to be placed in the prison with the rest of your company."

***

Never in my short life, did I imagine that I would be in the same dungeon, behind the same doors, and resting on the same wooden beds for a second time in a row. At least it wasn't as full the second time around.

"Any idea why your sword is doing that?" I asked Timmore, noticing the sword was pointing to the wall behind us.

"Not a clue," he admitted.

"Well, this is a first," Rathaetouy said giving a sigh, "I can now check off 'rotting behind bars' on my bucket list."

"Hey, Sir Wilhelm is doing his best," Timmore said defensively, "Not his fault Dhikrullah took over everything and started killing creatures."

"Where's Berry?" I asked noting his absence.

"R-r-r-ight here," he answered stuttering up a storm, "S-s-sorry but, I-I-'ve had too much excitement for one day."

*Poor kid* I thought, I knew exactly where he was coming from. It took all my strength to push the horrific, mangled expression on the guard's face to the furthest corners of my brain. At least here everyone's paws were tied, and no one could hurt us.

"This is so weird," Timmore said commenting on his sword, "Look at this, every time I turn this way and that, see?"

Berry watched it, and he looked like he was about to say something but didn't have the strength to.

"It's probably pointing to where the diamond is," Rathaetouy suggested.

"So, the diamond is in the castle," I said recollecting on where I last saw a diamond. For a castle, I should have remembered seeing a diamond somewhere, but I couldn't.

"W-w-ait a second," Berry said speaking up, "G-g-guys gather around me."

We did what he wanted and we all waited to hear what he had to say.

"W-w-we need to get out here," he continued, "We can u-use Melvin's Sword to c-cut this rope, g-g-get out of this place, a-and look for the emerald."

It was the only idea we had for the time. But there were a lot of things we were unsure of, such as; how were we supposed to escape and not get caught?

"L-lets trying c-cutting our bonds," Berry whispered to us. It was not easy trying to free ourselves in secret while surrounded by thugs and ruffians.

"Hold on," Rathaetouy commented, "Why are we doing this in the first place? I was never told why we need the sword, or why we need the diamonds. Why give Dhikrullah what he wants in the first place?"

"We need him to make the wish first," I reminded him.

The sword cut through Ratheatouy's ropes. It was then when we decided to keep our paws through the holes of the wooden boards, in order not to get the attention of the other inmates.

Berry's ropes were the next to go, and it was my turn soon but then we heard a knock at the door.

"Psss...." a voice whispered through the bars. We all looked to where the voice was coming from. Who did we see, but Gaheeto poking his head up.

"Wilhelm," he said, "May I speak with you?"

"Sure," I said with curiosity.

"Okay," he answered, "Let me just unlock the door. Guard can you please leave us?"

I turned around facing the boys.

"When he opens the door, I'll see if I can slip you guys through," I explained to them. "Doesn't seem it will work," Rathaetouy said skeptically, "But it is the only plan we got."

The door was unlocked, and it opened with a slight crack.

"Alright Wilhelm, come with me," Gaheeto announced, before turning around and walking past from view.

Once we were all out, I thought it best to close the door, letting the prisoners out would definitely throw a wrench into our plans. The three boys stayed in the hallway, and I made my way around the corner where Gaheeto was waiting.

"So, what do you want to talk to me about cousin?" I asked him.

"Let's take a walk Wilhelm," he suggested. As we walked down the familiar corridor, I heard tiny footsteps behind us getting father and father away.

"Mind explaining why my best knight was mutilated tonight?" he asked me.

"That was all Dhirkulla's not mine or the boy's." I said.

"So you just so happen to be conveniently standing behind the animal that killed my guards?" Gaheeto asked.

"You got to believe me." I begged, "I'm your cousin!"

'Wilhelm, I didn't break you out to talk about Dhirkullah," he said nearly shouting without raising his voice. 'I broke you out because I need to talk to you about Rudding."

After seconds of silence, I spoke up.

"Why?" I asked.

"I'm not the one ruling Rulksferd," Gaheeto said with his head to the ground. "Sure, I have the title, I have the crown, I have the throne; but it's Rudding who's doing all the work.

He's been telling me what to do ever since day one! I had a whole slew of ideas to turn this place around, but no, everything has to be his way."

"He is the advisor after all."

"But didn't you think it odd how he was the only one, other than you, in the court room with me? The first time I sat on the throne, I had all your advisors, all of them. But then, one by one, they disappeared, until Rudding was left."

My ears picked up. The worst fears of mine were coming to light again.

"I knew he was behind it somehow, I just couldn't prove it," he continued, "But I dare not speak against him, unless he would kill me too. Thank goodness our conquering of kingdoms has been diplomatic, I would have no choice but to go to war otherwise."

"How many kingdoms have you conquered already?"

"Only three so far. My own, Partajin, and Geval. But it's only a matter a time before one kingdom holds back, and Rudding will force me to attack. I don't want to rule like this Wilhelm. I don't even want to live this way. So that is why I'll give you the permission to kill me."

"What?"

"Here, take my dagger, and stab me with it."

"Gaheeto, no. We'll find a way; we'll find the proof against Rudding. If I kill you, you'll just make things worse."

"There is no other way, do you think if there was a way, I would have used it?"

He placed the dagger in my paw.

"I can't do it Gaheeto," I begged him, "If you're that scared of him, why don't you kill him yourself?"

"I don't know who's loyal to whom," Gaheeto cried. "If I kill Rudding, how do I know a knight or a guard won't kill me. I don't know what to do, Wilhelm. I'm trapped; I want out!"

I tired calming him down, I told him to take deep breaths and think.

"So, you want out?" we heard someone say, "I can arrange that."

We turned around. A slash came out of nowhere hitting Gaheeto. A fresh cut red appeared across his chest. From the shadows, we saw him standing proud with a sword in his paws.

"The only way out, is to do what I say," said Rudding, "Don't worry, it's merely a flesh wound, nothing major. But if you defy me once again, it will become more than that, I assure you."

"Leave him alone, Rudding," I said pushing my cousin to the side. "If you want to go through him, you'll have to go through me."

"You?" he asked offended, "As I recalled, it was you who was running away from a mob. A mob that was created by your doing. I'm not scared of you. Plus, it seems like your paws are tied."

"My paws might be tied," I said glaring at him, still holding on to the dagger, "And I might have been a coward before, but I will kill you now."

"Go ahead," he said mockingly, "This should be fun."

I ran towards him, giving what I imagined what a warrior's scream would be. Out of nowhere, I was held back. Rudding looked startled, but not because of me.

"I hate to interrupt a good fight," Dhikrullah said announcing his presence, "But there's a front row seat to my victory, and this, simpleton, has his name written all over it, good day."

With that the hallway, the tapestries, and Rudding vanished from my eyes. What stood in front of me was something I dreamed I would never see again. The very thing that killed the first of my brothers towered over me like the gates to death itself.

# Chapter XXii

*Has this always been here?* I thought to myself. I distinctly remember my father burning the merry-go-round as soon as my first brother died. Even the porcelain horses were enough to give me unwanted memories.

I heard muffle screams, behind me. I turned around to see Berry, Rathaetouy, and Timmore but in a terrifying state. Their mouths were completely gone, as if they were never born with a mouth, and their paws were turned into stubs.

"At first, I wanted to kill them," Dhikrullah, "But then I realized, what would be the fun in that?"

"Well you should have thought through your plan. How are you supposing to find the diamond without Timmore's help?"

His grin grew wider, and he pointed to the top of the ride. There it rested with pride, for the entire world to see, the final diamond.

"How do figure of getting up there?" I asked him.

From his robe, he pulled out the wand, and poofed the magic bag into existence. Out of the bag he pulled a tiny pouch and dumped the contents onto his feet.

His body started floating. He floated past the white, shiny horses, and onto the red and yellow big top, all while holding one to the magic bag.

He rested his feet and smirked.

"It's amazing what you can do when you have magic on your side," he told me. "Really, you should try it sometime."

Before picking up the diamond, he took out the Ynjusay from within the bag, and laid it down. He placed the black diamond onto the final candle holder and gave out a laugh.

"I can't wait!" he said giddily. "I'm so close."

He then took out the Boar's genie lamp and was about to say the magic words. But then, he gasped. I couldn't help but give out a chuckle.

"You've forgot the magic words, haven't you?" I said grinning ear to ear.

"No, I haven't," he denied.

"Then say them, what are you waiting for?"

He said some random words, that didn't even sound close to what I heard from the cave. Needless to say, the words had no effect.

"It's over Dhikrullah," I said victoriously. "You lost, we won."

"No, it's far from over!" he yelled back at me. "I'll. . ."

The edge a of sword thrust through his chest. We all jumped back with horror. Dhikrullah dropped everything and fell flat on the roof, his blood leaking onto the floor of the ride.

What happened next was hard to describe. It was as if a curtain from another reality was being lifted. Attached to the sword was a paw; then, out of nowhere, another paw poked out. The paw went into the air and pulled something down, something invisible.

There he was, Uknamra, with a sword in his right paw, and the invisible cloak in his left.

The magical bag disappeared the same way it had appeared. Berry, Rathaetouy, and Timmore got their mouths and paws back.

Dhikrullah turned his head around, and was about to scream, but he was either losing his strength or the blood was filling his lungs.

"But I thought, I killed you," he said gagging.

"You thought, *you thought*," Uknamra said chucklingly, "Well, now you know where you failed. Actually, you failed on many occasions. Shall I list them all?"

"I don't understand."

"Let's see, not only did you fail to confiscate all of the magical items, didn't you think it strange how I seemed to not sense the magic lamp in the cave when you had that rat tied?"

"I'm actually a lemming, but pretty close," I clarified.

Dhikrullah gave out one last scream in frustration, before his final breath left his lips.

"Nice betrayal, Uknamra," I said cynically. "There's this beaver I know, and you would really get along with him."

"You know nothing shrew," he said turning his head towards me. "He was the one who betrayed me. I'm merely getting my revenge."

"Revenge for what?" Timmore asked picking up his sword.

"He stole my plan for his own. I was the only one who knew Kharull used the magic of a genie. I was trying to collect the pieces for the Ynjusay, but Kharull's spell kept forcing me to worship him. It was so humiliating. It was like I was trapped in my own body. I could only watch myself bow down for his every desire."

As spewed out his monologue, I searched for a way to get on top of the merry-go-round.

"I was lucky to survive the raids he'd sent us on. But when Kharull died, it made such a hole within the group. Everyone thought being free was a bad thing, but I was the only one who thought otherwise. I shared my plans with Dhikrullah, who was once my only friend. I guess he saw that through the Ynjusay he could bring the rule of Kharull back."

"So, you wanted to become Kharull yourself?" I asked him, inching closer to the amusement ride.

"You catch on quick, mouse. Now if you excuse me, I have a wish to make."

He held the lamp high, and uttered the same phrase, with the same "ohs," "ahs," and "kuhs."

Black smoke came out of the genie lamp and into the vacant diamond. He tossed the genie lamp to the floor, almost hitting me square on the head.

He picked up the Ynjusay with both paws.

"Genies," he announced, "I wish to have the rule, of the entire Valley, even greater than the rule of Kharull."

A bolt of lightning hit one emerald diamond the other, lighting them up one by one. There was no way to stop it.

A breeze had picked up, forcing the platform of the dormant ride to move. The room ceiling became as bright as the sun, while giving a purple tint to the walls. I couldn't look away. The room felt like it was spinning along with the horses on the ride.

"Bear witness!" Uknamra announced. "Of the rule of Uknamra the Great!"

The doors behind us were forced open. Gaheeto and Rudding stood their dumbfounded.

I couldn't hear their voices over the wind but I think they both said something on the lines of, "What's going on here?"

The uncanny horses were now blurs. Uknamra lost his balance, and fell to the ground, taking the

Ynjusay with him. Dhikrullah fell into the merry-go-round. Sounds of his body tossing and turning, preluded the mess the servants would have to clean up. The ground met Uknamra with a bone-shattering thud. His limp body was dragged by the wind. His claws dug into the floor, desperately trying to hold on to something.

The diamonds bounced out of their holders, and the wind forced them to roll in different directions. Steam came out of each diamond as the winds calmed down slowing the merry-go-round. The celestial body faded away and everything went completely, absolutely still.

# CHaPTER XXiii

Uknamra rubbed his head and looked around with his mouth wide open.

"I don't understand," he said perplexed. "Nothing happened."

"How would you know?" I asked cunningly. "Seems to me your wish was granted."

"But how come I don't see it? Why aren't all of you bowing down before me?"

"Maybe you should have made your wish more specific Uknamra," the four genies said at once, rising from the emeralds like steam. The Great Mighty Boar was too excited about his freedom to say anything.

"You should have known, Uknamra," I said stepping towards him. "When genies grant wishes, they do it in ways you won't expect."

Uknamra fell to his knees and cursed himself for being so foolish.

Each genie was overjoyed for their new-found freedom. The Great Mighty Boar floated straight through the wall with excitement, not even bothering with the rest of us. I was just happy for Helina, who was free at last. We ran to each other's grasps, with smiles on our faces.

"Helina, come on!" said Esmeralda towards the ceiling. "Our eternal reward is awaiting us."

"You can't go," I told her. "You're the first creature that ever cared about me. Without you, none of this would have been possible."

She placed her translucent finger on top of my lips.

"No, Wilhelm," she said, while her mouth weakly tried to keep a smile, "I wasn't the only one. Turn around. These three boys have stuck with you. They're the ones who have made you the creature you are today. In death we will be separated, but even then, I'll continue to care for you and love you."

She floated away with the rest of the genies, despite my begging her to stay.

It was Timmore who placed his paw onto my shoulder, then Berry, and finally Rathaetouy. I didn't want her to go, but what could I do? However, in a way,

Helina wanted to be free, and now she was. Why was I crying? Shouldn't I have been happy for her?

"Goodbye, Wilhelm," she said as her body went through the heavens above. "I'll cherish our adventure for all eternity."

And just like that she was gone, never to be seen again. I fell to my knees; my paws were the only thing keeping my head from hitting the floor. That's where I mourned the disappearance of Helina, my first good friend.

Suddenly, a scream could be heard from down the hallway.

The Great Mighty Boar was being dragged through the stone walls. His paws would have scratched the floor if he wasn't translucent.

"No, I can't go back!" he pleaded, to whom I don't know. "Do you know what He'll do to me? He'll send me back to the Seventh Underground! I don't want to go back! How about I demand agriculture sacrifices instead of animal sacrifices?"

Despite all his pleading and begging, nothing seemed to protect him from the force sucking him right into the ceiling, and that was the last we had ever saw of him.

Uknamra launched himself towards Timmore's sword and grasped his knee.

"Kill me," he begged. "Kill me now just do it!"

"I, I can't," Timmore said in utter terror.

"Get your dirty paws off of him!" Rathaetouy shouted.

"You stay out of this!" Uknamra said lashing out his dagger. He missed Rathaetouy by an inch. Rathaetouy tackled him to the ground.

Uknamra gave out one last groan. Rathaetouy got up, revealing the dagger, firmly placed in Uknamara's chest.

"I'm sorry," he said, "It had to be done.

"Could someone please tell me what's going on here?" Rudding asked finding his voice. "You creatures have some questions to answer."

"So, do you Rudding!" Gaheeto said from behind.

As if on cue one of guards tied the Rudding's paws up. Rudding turned around, "You can't do this; you don't even have a charge against me."

"Conspiracy against the emperor," Gaheeto answered.

"Where's your proof?"

"You attempted to murder me, for one."

"You said that you wanted out," he said stammering, "I was just. . . you know."

"Yeah, that's what I thought," Gaheeto said with a smirk while crossing his arms, "Guards, take him away!"

\*\*\*

You think I would have spent my time celebrating, but instead I was back to the damp, depressing and dark prison. Not that I had gotten myself in trouble or anything but for curiosity sake.

Rudding looked up.

"What do you want?" he asked me. "Come to humiliate me some more?"

"I need some answers," I told him. "Like what were you up to, and why?"

He gave a sigh.

"What you probably understand is by now, is that the Valley is so much larger than Rulksferd," he explained, "Such a variety among creatures, ideas, and beliefs that have caused war and division among our Valley. Do you have any idea what we could accomplish if we were united as one? I wanted to be at the forefront of the unification of the Valley. Ah, so close, yet so far."

"Why you? What makes you so important?"

He chuckled.

"Wouldn't you like to know. I have connections, friends in high places you could say. Just you They'll free me, just you wait. Once they free me, they'll come after you and your friends."

I had the feeling he wouldn't reveal anything else to me. I didn't even give him the pleasure of a goodbye. Closing the door, I was left with the memory of him rotting in that prison, and that was alright with me.

***

It was day four since I had returned to Rulksferd, and it made me forget what it was like to rest on a leaf of a tree, a bed on a pirate ship, or in a guest room inside a monastery.

I walked onto the balcony, of the west wing of the castle, to take in the view. Despite the village in shambles, the yellow morning sun, and the golden clouds made it quite a sight to behold.

"Pretty amazing, I know," I heard Gaheeto say from behind me. "The village still needs work though."

"You've done a good job so far."

"Nah. That was all Rudding. I just did what he asked, like a mindless puppet."

The rush of the cool winds brushed through the trees. The villagers came out of their houses and began to do their daily chores. I took time observing their routines, for it was the first time I saw the common folk in action (when they weren't ordering my head on a platter that is).

"I'm going to be leaving Rulksferd," my cousin said with a deep breath. "And I don't think I'll ever return."

"But you're the emperor, the creatures need you!" I told him.

"I told you I didn't want to be emperor. I was thinking, since you're here now, you could rule in my place."

"I was a terrible leader," I told him. "There's no way they'll want to elect me."

"Under normal circumstances yes, but what I have planned might change that," my cousin said with a wink.

"You're not going to try to kill yourself again."

"Nothing of the sort. In fact, I did some research on those slippers in the castle library, and I think I have just the thing to make everyone happy."

\*\*\*

*This is stupid* I thought to myself *There's no way this will work.*

Timmore, Berry, Rathaetouy and I stood against the wall of the gate to the castle. My cousin was about to make his big announcement to everyone in Rulksferd. I was not used to seeing this many creatures not wanting me to be drawn and quartered. A big, green hot air balloon sat by the castle gates.

The crowd murmured amongst themselves before the buglers gave their cry of fanfare.

"The Great Emperor of Rulksferd approaches!" a squire announced. The crowd cheered. My cousin walked out of the gate theatrically.

"My fellow creatures!" he began, "It has come to my attention that there has been a conspiracy against me, your emperor!"

The crowd mumbled with concern.

"I must go into hiding, in order to protect myself and all of you," he continued. "I wish there was some other way, but alas, it is my burden to bear."

I slowly turned away, not taking any chances.

"In conclusion, I pronounce that Wilhelm IV will be Emperor of Rulksferd during my absence."

He grabbed me by the shoulder and dragged me to face the villagers, who gave me evil stares.

"Why him?" shouted an angry rabbit.

"He caused nothing but trouble!" shouted a hamster.

"He made stupid laws!" cried an angry dormouse.

The accusations grew. They began to boo and threw mud and food at me.

"Listen," my cousin said bringing order back to the crowd. "I know my cousin is not well liked around you folks, but desperate times call for desperate matters. Keep in mind, he will be ruling on my behalf. Whatever you do, do not lay a paw on even a single strand of his fur. An attack against Wilhelm is an attack against me."

The villagers began giving disgruntled comments amongst themselves.

"Now if you don't mind, I really should be going," my cousin said abruptly. "Goodbye to you all, and be kind to my cousin Wilhelm."

The crowd begged him not to leave, but Gaheeto and I knew it was too late to back down now.

With some help from the castle servants, my cousin took off in his hot air balloon.

"Emperor Gaheeto, don't leave!" cried a squirrel.

"Please come back!" shouted another.

"I can't!" Gaheeto shouted from above. "Besides, I don't know how it works. Goodbye to you all, goodbye!"

And with that he floated into the sky and above the clouds, never to be seen again.

Dead silence followed. I had to say something.

"Well, so, how have you guys been?" I asked awkwardly.

"What's stopping us from killing him right now?" a gerbil asked - I later learned his name was Gregory - demanding to know the answer.

"We are," said the knights slightly revealing their swords. "Emperor Gaheeto's orders, remember?"

Gregory glanced at the knight, before staring back at me.

"You might be the Emperor's replacement," he said gritting his teeth. "But you ain't no emperor of mine."

He stormed off in a huff, and, to the rest of the villagers, that was the end of it.

# CHAPTER XXIV

And that, my dear readers, was how I was I dethroned and become Emperor of Rulksferd. Now hold on, don't close the book yet. There are still several things I need to wrap up.

Although you would think my first order of business would be to attend to the re-construction of the village, I had to go back to Blue Wall Abbey, I had to know if the other kids and my brother were safe.

I, along with Timmore, Berry, Rathaetouy and a few knights took off for the Abbey at first light the following day.

"There he is!" said a voice that I knew all too well. There was Gregory standing on a top of the hill next to the side of the rode, and it appeared that he had a few friends with him.

"Abandoning us already?" he yelled at us, while his girl badger friend through a tomato at my horse.

"Oy!" exclaimed one of the knights, "Assaulting the Emperor is a capital offense."

"He isn't my emperor," she said in a huff.

"Why don't you come down here yourselves you cowards," Rathaetouy screamed.

"Them's fighting words," Gregory replied, with his two friends laughing in unison.

"Rathaetouy come on," I told him, "Let's try to ignore them."

And that's exactly what we did. They kept throwing rocks and pebbles at us, but after a few less than flattery remarks, they finally gave up and called it a day.

\*\*\*

When we arrived at the abbey, the walls were still pristine as always, but the deadly silence was too unnerving for my taste. I got off my horse, walked towards the door, and knocked on it with my bare knuckles. There was nothing else we could do but wait, and wait we did.

A little snout popped up from above the wall. Friend or foe, we were about to find out.

"Brother Wilhelm you're back!" my brother exclaimed. "Hold on. Brother Jon, Brother Ruppert, open the doors."

Seconds later, two *thwunks* could be heard and the doors slowly creaked opened. Brother Jon was a giant rat with large arm muscles, and Brother Ruppert was just as big and strong as Brother Jon. Both of the monks had burnt robes and had bandages on all of their arms and foreheads. Brother Ruppert offered to take our horses to the stable, to which we all accepted.

It appeared that the front section of Blue Wall was left untouched by the chaos of the night so long ago. I was in Hallway C when I met my brother once again.

"Oh, youngest brother Wilhelm," he said with a warm embrace. His robes were burnt, and some of his fur on his left cheek was scratched out.

"Sorry for our drab appearance," he continued. "We've been so busy trying to rebuild, we haven't had a chance to change our garments."

The further along the abbey we went, the worse the abbey became. The walks became black with brunt marks, parts of the ceiling were slanting downward, pouring the contents of the second floor to the first floor. Burnt and unsteady beams and planks were poking out, making me wonder why the floor above us didn't collapse and squish us like bugs.

The garden where the abbey held its feasts was completely burnt away. Not a single strand of green could be seen. I looked to my left to see the now destroyed wall where I had once shot arrows from, or at least tried to.

I could barely take it all in when I heard "Sir Wilhelm!" by several happy and familiar voices.

To my joyful relief, the gang of kids I shared my adventure with, were safe and sound. True, they looked rough around the edges, but they were alive and well none the less.

"We missed you, Wilhelm!" said Samuel II

"I told ya he would come back," said Rob.

After giving a group hug, they greeted Timmore and Berry with cheerful enthusiasm. We could have filled the sea with our overwhelming sense of happiness we all shared. But it made Rathaetouy's absence even more apparent.

"Sir Wilhelm," said an old whispery voice. I turned behind me to see Montague holding a mace in his paws.

"Oh, hi, Montague," I said afraid he would accidently drop the thing on my head.

"You should have been here," he said with a smile on his face. "Once our invaders realized their leaders abandoned, they started turning on one another. It was amazing!"

He looked towards the sky with pleasure before continuing.

"Some left for the ocean and some ran away, but a small few stayed behind offering themselves for eternal servitude, can you believe it?"

"No, I can't," I said unable to keep myself from looking at Stonegrave, now towering behind him.

"Welcome back, Sir Wilhelm," he said under his breath.

"Hello again, Stonegrave," I said expecting him to shake my paw, but he never did.

"I just want to apologize for the way I treated you," he said struggling to pronounce each syllable. "My stubbornness, pride and fear clouded my better judgment. But, just so we're clear, don't tell anyone I said this to you, understand?"

"I understand," I replied. "Thank you."

"Don't mention it," he said.

"You know what you did!" I heard a familiar voice in the distance. I scanned the area trying to find him. It wasn't long until I finally spotted Rathaetouy arguing with my brother. I could not hear what they were saying, but from their faces it wasn't a happy reunion.

Rathaetouy curled his fingers, as if he were about to choke my brother, and violently moved them up and down. My brother had his paws opened, and his body shrank with each outburst from Rathaetouy.

Once Rathaetouy calmed down for a bit, my brother tried to reach out to him, but Rathaetouy stormed off in the other direction.

My brother, brushing his eyes, slowly walked towards us.

"Now," he said with a sniff, "What can we do for you brother?"

"Actually it's, what can I do for you?" I corrected.

"You're too kind, brother," he said. "Come to think of it, we need more supplies. Bricks and mortar don't grow on trees you know."

"Once I return to my castle, I'll make sure to send enough bricks and mortar to build a new abbey."

My brother gave a small chuckle, right before my boys ganged up on me. To this, his chuckle became a laugh.

"Is it true that you're now a king Sir Wilhelm?" Simon I asked.

"Actually, I am an emperor," I told them.

"Can we stay in your palace?" they began to ask.

"Well, I'll have to get the place prepared for you guys first," I replied.

"How about you go back to your palace, and once you're ready we'll send the boys over there," my brother suggested.

"That's not a bad idea," I remarked, "not a bad idea at all."

\*\*\*

My knights, Rathaetouy, and I got on our horses and left Blue Wall Abbey just as the sun was about to set. Timmore and Berry decided to stay behind and catch up with their friends.

I was becoming concerned about Rathaetouy. He barely said a word, and his sharp grimace seemed to be frozen in place.

"Is there anything you want to talk about?" I said after directing my horse to trot beside his.

He gave a small *huff* under his breath.

"My brother was only doing what he thought was. . ."

"I don't want to talk about it," he snapped.

"You can't hold a grudge forever."

"Watch me."

"Rathaetouy, this is not like you."

"Well, I don't know what I'm like, okay? I don't know what I am supposed to be. I'm not a savior like Timmore. I'm not a hero like you. I'm a nobody."

The birds ceased their playful chirping.

"You're still a kid, Rathaetouy," I said looking into his eyes. "You have plenty of time to figure out who you want to be. And when you make a mistake, you'll be able to start over with a clean slate."

Suddenly, we were given a not so hearty welcome by Gregory and his friends, and their friends. Each word pierced my skin like an arrow, but I had no choice but to shake it off.

We arrived at the castle, closed the gates, guided the horses back into the stable, and went our separate ways. I didn't see where Rathaetouy headed off to, I just hoped he wouldn't do anything rash.

I walked up the stairs, and to my quarters. I stepped out onto the balcony, to watch the beautiful sunset.

The view was amazing, and it made me forget I was once a tyrannical ruler. I was given a second chance at life. I looked to the sky where I knew Helina was watching me from and swore to her that I would be a ruler she would be proud of.

# ACKNOWLEDGEMENTS

It takes a village to raise a child, and the same can be said for this book. *Wilhelm* would not have been possible if it weren't for these amazing people! I would like to thank Gary T. Val and Nathaniel Long for making the illustrations for this book. I would like to thank my beta readers Caleb Battle, Emily Ayers, Hanna Buwalda, and Robert Ring, for reading through it and giving me suggestions along the way. I would like to thank my parents for supporting me and doing their best to promote this book. I want to thank Andrew Morison for his amazing voice work. I want to thank God for giving me the talent of storytelling. And finally, I want to thank you, dear reader, for giving *Wilhelm* a read, you don't know how much it means to me. Thank you.

-W.R.L. Battle (06/02/2021)

# ABOUT THE AUTHOR

**W.R.L. BATTLE** started writing when he was a little a kid. He currently resides in a small town in South Carolina, surrounded by friends and family. He has written several short stories, which can be found on Reedsy.com. *Wilhelm* is his first novel.

Made in the USA
Columbia, SC
14 July 2021